He's always been the One

L.L. Diamond

He's Always Been the One

By L.L. Diamond

Published by L.L. Diamond

Copyright ©2021 LL Diamond

Cover and internal design © 2021 L.L. Diamond
Cover design by L.L. Diamond/Diamondback Covers
Cover Art Loving Couple at Park by Jacob Lund and Fireflies by the River in the Night by Sun God via Shutterstock

ISBN-13: 978-1-7342783-9-2

Facebook: https://www.facebook.com/LLDiamond
Instagram: @l.l.diamond
Twitter: @LLDiamond2
Blog: http://lldiamondwrites.com/
Austen Variations: http://austenvariations.com/

Other works by L.L. Diamond include:
Rain and Retribution
A Matter of Chance
An Unwavering Trust
The Earl's Conquest
Particular Intentions

Chapter 1

The couple seated across the desk from me was young, very young—high school sweethearts, who had only just graduated from the University of South Carolina and were finally tying the knot. The groom's affectionate smile while he tenderly held his fiancée's hand spoke of a contentment I'd yet to know and caused my chest to ache.

The stars in their eyes reminded me of a portrait of my parents that adorned the mantel in my grandmother's house. Like the twosome in front of me, the pair in the picture was a young interracial couple who'd had more to overcome thirty years ago than, hopefully, the couple in front of me.

While I'd worked for Forever Yours Wedding Planners for several years, planning weddings on my own was still a new role, so I concentrated on appearing confident. I did know what I was doing. After all, I'd assisted Jena, Ellie, and Charlie often enough to understand how the process worked.

I settled back into my chair and picked up my pen to make a note on the small pad I always kept at the ready. "Okay, we've nailed down the church and the venue for the reception. Have you made your guest list yet?" They shook their heads. "I need you to prepare it soon so I can contact caterers and bakeries for estimates on the food and the cake. Do you have any ideas for the menu? That might help me narrow down which caterer would better suit your needs."

A gentle knock at my office door caused us all to turn as Jena, one of my employers, peeked inside. "I'm sorry for the interruption. Maggie, your grandmother's on the phone. She says it's urgent."

My heart dropped like a fifty-pound weight, and I froze solid for a second or two. Gram *never* called me at work. She was one of the most independent people I'd ever known. Something had to be wrong, very wrong. I lunged forward and picked up the office phone. "Gram?"

"Maggie! Thank goodness! I tried your cell, but it went straight to voicemail."

My stomach twisted and my muscles tensed into knots. Her voice was breathless and dramatic. My grandmother was *never* dramatic. "I'm with a client, so my phone's on silent. What's wrong?"

"Oh, I'm so sorry for interrupting. I swear I wouldn't have called unless it was important." Her pitch had risen as she spoke. With Jena getting married in two weeks and Charlie ready to pop with her first child, I'd been given more responsibility. I knew the last thing my grandmother wanted was to interrupt me while I worked.

"I know that, Gram. I need you to tell me what's going on?"

"I fell on that bad wood on the back steps." I inhaled sharply, but before I could say a word, Gram jumped in. "I was running out to fetch Harper when it happened. I'm sorry. I tried calling Mrs. Bunting next door and your friend Mei. Neither answered."

I held up my hand. "I can pick up Harper, but what about you? Are you okay?"

Her voice resumed her usual no-nonsense tone but remained tight. "I'll be fine, dear. I don't think I'm hurt. You take care of Harper and don't worry about me."

"You know I'm going to worry until I see you for myself. I'll be home as soon as I can."

My grandmother's huff was as clear as day through the line. "Margaret Jane Dashwood, finish what you need to at work. I'll be fine. Now, go pick up your daughter."

"Yes, ma'am."

Gram hung up, and I placed the receiver on the base as I peered around at everyone now watching me. "I'm so sorry. I have to go." I grabbed my purse from under the desk and looked toward Jena. "Would you mind scheduling the next appointment for Lydia and Greg? Would two weeks work?" I asked the couple. "You can bring in your initial guest list so we have that ball park figure for estimates and menu selection."

Jena stepped around my desk and gently pressed me toward the door. "We'll figure it out. Please call and let me know if your grandmother is well, or if you need anything."

"Thanks." I extended my hand to Lydia. "I'm so sorry."

The young woman waved me off before she took my hand. "Don't worry about it. I hope it's nothing serious."

"Thank you." I shook Greg's hand quickly before I hurried through the door.

As soon as I exited the historic red brick home that housed our offices, I jogged across the street as carefully as my heel-clad feet could carry me into the park, slowing to a brisk walk as I followed the pathway towards the pond.

In no time, my silk tank began sticking to me. September weather in South Carolina was never predictable. The weather could cool a little early or the scorching heat of August could carry through until November if Mother Nature felt more than a little capricious. Since this was merely the first week of

September, we still had the heat rather than a quick relief from the higher summer temperatures.

I pulled my phone from the side pocket of my purse and pressed a button for the time. I had five minutes to get to Marysville Elementary before the final bell, and probably another two or three minutes before Harper came barreling through the front doors looking for Gram. Driving had been out of the question since traffic around the school was hellacious at this time of day. The last thing I wanted to deal with was those holier than thou mothers who volunteered for car pick-up. I never knew why they gave me the evil eye, and frankly, I ceased to care a long time ago. Instead, I boycotted the Marysville mom mafia. Don't get me wrong, I volunteered in the classrooms when I had a day off, and I provided any supplies the teachers requested. I simply didn't need to socialize with a bunch of superficial, hoity-toity society belles to help out at the school.

The bell rang not long after I joined the throng of parents waiting in the designated spot for school pick up. Within seconds, children began pouring from the doors like a flash flood, and a minute later Harper's dark red space buns flew through the center of the surge until she saw me. She stopped and a huge smile lit her face. "Mommy!" She bounded forward and grabbed my hand. "Where's Gram?"

"She fell on the back stairs, so as soon as we make it back to the office and get the car, we're going to have to go home and see if she's hurt." We turned and began walking back toward the park, which was the quickest path between the two points. "Did you do anything fun at school today?"

"Mrs. Traub brought in a guinea pig for us to take care of. His name's Herschel."

"Herschel?"

"Yeah, his little nose does this when he eats lettuce." She wiggled her little freckled nose in the cutest way, and I laughed.

"He does?"

"Can we get a guinea pig?"

"You said you wanted a kitten like Bacon. Would you really rather have a guinea pig?" I'd taken her to the office once on a Saturday to pick up a file, and she fell in love with Jena's little calico ball of fluff. Of course, Bacon wasn't so little anymore, but she was still adorable and full of kittenish mischief. I hoped Harper would change her mind on the guinea pig. I did not want an over-grown rat in the house.

"Can't we have both? Gram won't mind. She likes animals. She's always telling me stories about growing up on her daddy's farm."

"We'll see." We hurried across the street as I clicked the button on my key to unlock my more than a decade old crossover. My car wasn't flashy, but it was reliable and not an eyesore when I needed to transport clients.

Once Harper was buckled in the back, I carefully pulled out and started for home. "I'm simply not sure about having an animal yet. It's a lot of responsibility."

"I can feed it. It could sleep in my bed."

"Harp, a guinea pig wouldn't sleep all night in your bed. A cat wouldn't even sleep with you the entire night because they like to roam around. At least a cat would be easier to find in the morning." That wasn't even taking into account vet bills, food, kitty litter, or shavings for a cage. I'd made decent money the last few years as an assistant in the office, but Jena, Charlie, and Ellie had recently given me the opportunity to be more—to actually plan weddings instead of helping and answering phones. Yes, the pay was better so I'd hoped to start a college fund for Harper and purchase a newer car, not get a pet.

In less than five minutes, we'd pulled into the garage behind the house. Like the office, my grandmother's home was located in the historic district of Marysville. I loved the old brick homes and vast front porches—although Gram's was off an alley and had no front porch. Another benefit of living downtown was being within walking distance to anything we needed, though I drove to work in the event I needed to run an errand in Charleston or one of the surrounding small towns.

I helped Harper grab her Stitch backpack and lunchbox. If there was one thing my little girl adored, it was anything Lilo and Stitch. I'd had to search this style online. The star struck look on her face when she saw it was worth the effort. Thank heavens for Ebay!

I steered my daughter around the car to the door that led to the backyard. No sooner had we stepped through than Gram came into view, reclined on a stretcher on the back porch. A uniformed man stood on either side of her.

"Gram!" cried Harper, who broke into a run.

"You said you were okay." Yes, my voice held a tone of accusation. I really couldn't help it. She should've told me she was hurt. What if I'd decided to take Harper with me to work to finish as she'd suggested? She could've been sitting there for hours—except she didn't wait for me. She'd apparently handled matters herself.

"I didn't want to worry you." Gram winced as they carefully tightened a belt across her legs. Harper, meanwhile, had wheedled into a free space to hold Gram's hand. "It'll probably be the only time in my life I'm thankful for those dratted cell phones," she said in a weak laugh. "After I called you, I dialed 911, and in no time, these two handsome men showed up to take care of me."

The EMT with his back to me turned his head, his hazel eyes met mine, and I suddenly couldn't move my legs and my heart thrummed in this strange rhythm against my sternum. Elliot?

"Hi, Maggie."

Gram's face perked like a child when ice cream was mentioned. "Oh? Do the two of you know one another?" She'd been pushing me these last two years to do more than curl up on the sofa with a book on Friday nights. The last thing I wanted her to know was that I was acquainted with a hunky EMT.

"Elliot is friends with Charlie from work. They play volleyball together." I wasn't about to mention how the man could make me sweat faster than burpees in a sauna. My palms were already slick, and he hadn't said more than two words to me.

"We've got her ready to take her to the ER," said Elliot as they lifted the stretcher. He turned and pointed at the rotten wood steps leading off the porch. "If you can't fix that, they should be ripped out. They're dangerous—for all of you."

I bristled at his reprimand, regardless of how well-meaning it was. "I've planned on fixing them, but I've been busy at work. Where are you taking my grandmother?"

"Just to the local hospital." His partner stepped off the deck, and between the two of them, they gently lowered my grandmother off the porch. "We'd offer you a ride, but we only have room for one."

"It's fine. I need to see if Jena minds watching Harper so I can go. I'll be there as soon as I can, Gram."

"Take your time. It's not like I'm going to be ready to leave anytime soon." She dismissively waved me off; however, the grimace when she shifted clearly told how much pain she was trying to hide.

Harper and I followed them through the gate to the ambulance out front. Once Gram was loaded into the van with his colleague, Elliot placed a hand on my upper arm. "I'm no doctor, but I'd bet anything she's broken her hip. She might need surgery then rehabilitation once she's released. I normally don't tell family this much. I just don't want you to get caught off-guard when the doctors get the x-rays."

"Thanks. I appreciate it."

He squeezed my arm and leaned a hair closer, prompting a prickling of goosebumps across the back of my neck. "You might want to make that phone call to Jena. I'll see you later?"

"Sure," I said in this weird voice I'd never heard before. Why did I feel like a freshman in high school and the senior captain of the football team had smiled at me? I was a twenty-seven-year-old single mother, for Pete's sakes, not some dreamy young girl who'd never kissed a boy. That ship had sailed a long time ago.

"Is Gram going to be okay?"

Suddenly, what Elliot said hit me, and I squatted down beside Harper. "Let's go inside and pack Gram a bag before we go."

"Is she going to have to stay at the hospital?" Harper's wide eyes practically begged me to say no.

"She might. You need to remember that she'll be fine. You know how tough Gram is. You don't need to worry."

"Can we pack Stitch to keep her company?"

I smiled and squeezed her hand in mine. "Of course. Why don't you go and pick out which Stitch you think would be best."

Once we were inside, I grabbed an overnighter and put a few of Gram's nightgowns, under things, a toothbrush, toothpaste, and a brush inside and met Harper in the hall. "Are you ready?" She nodded while she clutched her favorite Stitch, the one with droopy ears and huge eyes, to her chest.

I loaded Harper back into the car, pulled up the office phone number, and pressed send, swapping my cell phone to speaker before I pulled out of the driveway.

"Forever Yours. This is Greta." Greta had originally worked part-time for the company helping at events. Since she'd graduated college and I'd been promoted, she'd started periodically working my former place at the front desk.

"Hi Greta, it's Maggie."

"Hi there. Jena told me you had to leave early. Is everything okay?"

"Kind of hectic at the moment. Is Jena available?"

Greta giggled. "She must have ESP because she just peered around the corner. Let me put you on hold so she can pick up."

After a bit, the line clicked. "You could've called my cell phone."

I stopped at the light and drummed my fingers on the steering wheel. "I didn't want to interrupt in the event you had a walk-in."

"Maggie, you've never called in sick, you've never had a family emergency until now, and you rarely bring Harper into the office, even though we've told you she's more than welcome whenever you need it. You wouldn't have left today if it wasn't important, so even in a meeting, I would answer. I'm sure the client would understand."

"Okay, got it." I took a deep breath as the light turned green, and I pressed on the gas pedal. "I need a favor. Gram may have broken her hip. After she called me, she called 911."

"Oh, crap!"

"Yeah, anyway, I can't bring Harper to the emergency room."

Before I could continue, Jena cut me off. "Bring her in. Let Aunt Jena spoil her rotten for a couple of hours. She can even spend the night if you need it."

"I didn't pack her a bag, and she has school tomorrow. The teacher usually sends home handwriting assignments that she might need help with. She's allergic to nuts. I have an epi-pen in my purse that I can leave with you. If you don't mind, please read the label on any food you might give her."

"No problem. I'll call Brandon. We can grill burgers and make home fries."

"She'll love that. Thank you."

"You've covered for us and always ensured we had help when we needed it. It's no bother. Any of us would be happy to help—even Charlie." Because she was due soon, Charlie was working from home unless she had a meeting. I was covering her weddings. "I've already let Ellie know your grandmother was sick, and she was going to pass the news along to Charlie. We're here for you. You can call any of us at any time. I hope you know that."

"I just pulled up in front."

"Gotcha," said Jena as the line clicked.

Twenty minutes later, I walked through the sliding electric doors of the emergency room. I'd have arrived earlier, but Jena had never used an epi-pen, so I gave her a quickie lesson before I left. In all fairness, Harper was fully capable of teaching Jena, however, my overprotective OCD niggle insisted I ensure it was done by me.

I strode up to the window, and the woman behind the desk shoved a panel open. "May I help you?"

"Yes, I'm here for Cordelia Dashwood. She was brought in by ambulance."

"Maggie!" I whipped around to Elliot, who held open a door to the side of the waiting room. He motioned for me to follow him. "I've got it, Leanne."

Without waiting for Leanne's permission, I hurried after Elliot. "Thank you."

We hurried down a corridor, and he motioned where I should turn down another hallway. "It's been pretty quiet here today. After giving your grandmother something for pain, they sent her straight down to radiology for x-rays. She shouldn't be too long. Do you want some coffee while you wait?"

"I'm good for the moment." I glanced back and forth around me. "Don't you need to go back to work?"

"No, I'm off, but I wanted to make sure you and your grandmother didn't need anything." He barked out a laugh and scratched the back of his neck. "That woman's a pistol. She asked me how old I am, where I live, and whether I had a 'young lady' in my life." He air-quoted "young lady."

My cheeks warmed. I already needed to wipe my sweaty palms down my skirt without Gram mortifying me. Why did she have to do that?

He shoved his hands in his pockets and glanced down to his feet. "Despite the efficiency of the local gossip mill, I hadn't realized you have a daughter."

"Oh?" I scraped my teeth along my bottom lip. "Perhaps because that's old news. Usually, I see you at the fitness center, work, or the grocery store, and I always make grocery runs on my way home from the office. Gram picks up Harper from school for me, so she's never with me. If we go somewhere, it's usually on weekends. Somehow, I doubt you frequent the Animal Forest or the aquarium."

After he chuckled, he shook his head. "No, those aren't my usual haunts." He cleared his throat. "Your grandmother is fairly active then?"

"She walks to school and back every day, helps keep the house clean, and cooks dinner most weekdays. She also quilts and sews. For eighty-two, she does pretty well."

"Being active will be good for her recovery."

We shifted to one side of the hallway for a nurse, pushing a patient in a wheelchair, to pass. "You don't have to wait with me, you know."

"What if I'd like to?"

I crossed my arms over my chest and leaned against the wall. It'd been so long since I'd even looked at a man. I had no clue what to do when Elliot made comments like that.

He stepped closer and nearly touched his shoulder to mine. "Are you sure you don't want that coffee?"

I watched my feet, avoiding his eye, while I tried to breathe away the butterflies and concentrate on what was important—Harper, Gram, my job in that order. I had no time to let whims and feelings get in the way. I may have liked Elliot Martin, yet I needed him to find another woman. I was still trying to understand why he seemed to be pursuing me. "We'll see," I said, wincing at how non-committal that sounded.

Chapter 2

I'd been languishing in the surgical waiting room since Gram was wheeled into surgery. For the past hour, I'd stared at the muted grey-blue walls that had been paired with that horrible blue, vinyl furniture that adorned nearly every waiting room in existence. The decorator had, no doubt, taken a class on calming colors, yet I still tapped my foot in a frantic rhythm on the floor. I swear time had crawled slower than a herd of turtles while I read and re-read the obligatory signs posted around the room, unwillingly committing them to memory. I blew out a breath and dropped my head to rest on the back of the sofa, putting the heels of my hands on my eyes. I'd tried to read a novel on my phone. My mind refused to cooperate so I was stuck, the practically sterile surroundings closing in on me.

"Coffee?"

My body jolted at the proximity of the low, familiar voice, and I removed my hands to find a coffee cup from Starlight café held in front of me. "How'd you know?"

"I checked in on your grandmother yesterday after my shift. She might've mentioned her surgery was today."

"Oh." That might've explained why Gram had given me that shit-eatin' grin yesterday. She could be devious when she wanted, though always for a good cause. I had to admit it was hard to stay angry with a five foot nothing elderly lady. She could give you some pathetic eyes capable of guilting even the iciest of hearts when she felt it necessary.

Elliot chuckled, a deep noise that rumbled through me. "She tried to persuade me to smuggle some whisky in for her."

"Geez, Gram," I muttered as I took the coffee. "She knows it's the last thing I'd do."

"Don't worry. I told her no. I didn't want to thin her blood before surgery."

"Thanks." I took a sip, waiting for the bite that comes from no milk or sugar of any kind, yet it never came. Instead, the perfect combination of milk, coffee, and hazelnut flavor rolled across my taste buds. "How'd you know?"

"I asked what you usually order. You know Miss Bates has the regulars' orders committed to memory."

"I don't always order the hazelnut."

He lifted one shoulder in a shrug. "She claimed you ordered the hazelnut more than any other flavor."

My eyes traced over his cleanly shaven jawline. I preferred the stubble, but he was still hot. "Do you have to work today?"

"No, I went into the gym earlier to work out, and now I'm here."

"You didn't have to come," I said softly. Shit! I sounded like such a bitch.

"I know. I wanted to." He dropped into a chair in front of me and propped his forearms on his knees. "Look, Maggie. I like you. I like you a lot. I've never really come out and said it before, so I am now."

"What about Harper?" My fingers tightened around the coffee as everything inside me clenched.

"What about her?"

I took another sip of coffee and rubbed my palm up and down the thigh of my jeans. Darned sweat! "Well, she's not exactly a guy magnet."

He frowned and shook his head. "Any guy who makes a kid his excuse is a douche canoe."

An amused bark burst from my throat. "I agree." His deep, warm laugh did strange things to my stomach. I closed my eyes, breathing evenly in the hopes it would stop. "I'm very flattered."

"Mags—"

I held up my hand. "You're a great guy, but I've busted my ass to build a life for Harper and me. I rarely have free time, and when I do, I spend all of it with my daughter and Gram."

He sat up and watched me with an odd dip of his eyebrows I couldn't interpret. "Don't you want to marry some day? Maybe have another child?"

"I fucked up my chance for that," I said quietly while I traced the letters on my cup with my finger. "I'm happy with the way things are. I'm not ready for them to change." I might wear out my vibrator in the next six months. A battery-operated boyfriend, however, didn't have the same demands as a living, breathing man. They also didn't leave. "I hope we can be friends."

"As a friend, am I allowed to try to change your mind?"

My head shook back and forth. "I'm not changing my mind."

He drank from his own cup before his eyes latched back onto mine. "Do I know Harper's father?"

"No, he doesn't live in Marysville anymore." I couldn't explain how I knew he would ask the history. Most people in Marysville remembered Sawyer from high school. Elliot hadn't grown up here, so he'd never met him. I suppose it was natural he would wonder. "I started dating Sawyer Crawford when I was sixteen. We stayed together through graduation, and we both decided to attend the College of Charleston. He was majoring in systems engineering, and I was majoring in art. When I learned I was pregnant and refused to have an abortion, he decided he wasn't ready to be a father. He'd hoped I would give the baby up for adoption. I simply couldn't do it. I loved her too much. That ended our relationship. Fortunately, his father's job was moved to Virginia shortly after we started college, so I don't have to deal with them either." That little detail was a blessing. His parents had always hated that Sawyer had "taken up" with me. I never knew what they hated about me. I only knew that they never wanted me around.

"Did you finish school?"

"Harper was born in June, so I was able to finish out my second year; however, even with Gram's help, I couldn't imagine trying to finish my degree full-time while being a single mom. For one thing, I needed a job of some kind to support us, and art classes are time consuming. Meanwhile, Gram's house needed some work, and she was struggling to pay for the repairs on her limited income. In the end, I changed my major to business administration and finished online. I also bartended and waited tables at Mugs in the evenings to pay bills and help out Gram."

"How did you end up wedding planning?"

"Jena, Charlie, and Ellie put out an ad for an assistant. Harper qualified for Head Start, so I dropped her off at school and Gram picked her up. I still worked at Mugs for nearly a year to save up some money. Tips were always good, so we were able to fix Gram's house and I was able to buy a decent car."

"Miss Dashwood?" I looked toward the doctor, who stood a few feet away.

I shot out of my chair and took a step forward. "Yes. How's Gram?"

"She came through surgery like a champ. She'll be monitored in recovery for an hour or so before she's moved back to her room. We'll need to watch her carefully for leg pain—more specifically thigh pain—for the next few weeks. The nurses should have her sitting up by this evening. Hopefully, we'll get her standing by tomorrow."

"So soon?" It sounded more painful than beneficial to me.

"Yes, we've found the sooner the better." The doctor smiled and glanced at the wall clock. "You might as well get something to eat since there's not much you can do before she wakes."

"Thank you," I said, holding out my hand to shake his.

"You're welcome. From the conversation I had with your grandmother's primary care doctor, she'll benefit from this procedure more than a lot of people her age. With a little rehabilitation and physical therapy, she should be able to resume her former lifestyle in time."

After saying "goodbye," the doctor walked away while everything in me sort of sagged, a large exhale leaving my lungs in a whoosh.

Elliot twitched his head toward the door. "Come on. Let's celebrate. I'll take you to lunch."

"Friends, Elliot."

His eyebrows shot up. "Friends take each other out to eat—especially after good news."

I cocked my head to the side and took stock of the man in front of me. Yes, I was the one who asked if we could be friends, but how much of a friendship could I handle with a man I was crazy attracted to? "Okay, sure. Why not?" Screw it. It was one lunch.

The hospital was on the outskirts of Marysville, though after its construction, a small community of businesses grew around it: a low-priced motel, a florist shop, a few medical supply companies, and a couple of restaurants—no doubt kept afloat by those who worked or convalesced in the hospital. The proximity to the medical complex made matters a lot more convenient.

Elliot led the way into a small place set on a corner. Outdoor seating begged for someone to enjoy warm air and sunshine, yet due to an overnight thundershower, no one braved the grey clouds to eat outside. Inside, a row of booths lined the windows while small tables were spread through the center of the room. A waitress invited us to seat ourselves, so Elliot walked backward for a few steps. "Where do you want to sit?"

"The booth that's open by the window looks good." It was still early for lunch, so while the restaurant had patrons, they weren't packed to the gills yet.

As soon as we seated ourselves, the waitress dropped two menus on the table and took our drink order before bustling away in the direction of the kitchen.

"How long have you been an EMT?"

He relaxed back into the shiny ivory vinyl while he fingered the roll of silverware on the table. "My parents didn't have the money for me to go to college, so I joined the Army

National Guard in high school to become an EMT. I went to school part-time after to complete my bachelor's degree. Three years ago, I started the physical therapy program at MUSC."

"Oh, wow," I said. "How much longer do you have?"

"I finished my coursework and clinicals last month and took my licensing exam two weeks ago. I'm just finishing out my last few weeks on the rig until my license comes in. I already have a job waiting for me."

"How long will it take for your license?"

"About four weeks."

"Congratulations."

He reddened a little and nodded. "Thanks. It's been a long road, but worth it."

"Are you still National Guard?"

"I am. Since I've finished physical therapy school, I'm now an officer. I've only got two more years before I hit my twenty years. I plan on retiring. I paid for physical therapy school myself so I wasn't obligated to stay any longer."

The waitress put our drinks in front of us, took our food order, and departed once more.

"You said you were an art major," he said. "Do you still draw or paint or whatever you did before Harper?"

"I sketched using powdered graphite and a brush, and no. I simply don't have the time." I shrugged and sighed. "I hated the classwork for my business degree, but it seemed more practical for a single mom. I love working with the Three Weddingteers because I can stretch those creative parts of my brain that haven't seen the light of day for so long."

He laughed and lifted his eyebrows. "The Three Weddingteers?"

I smiled in return. "I made the joke not long after I started working with them. It's kind of stuck."

He shook his head. "Who are your art heroes?"

"Art heroes?"

"Yes, who would you love to emulate? What artists speak to you?"

I crossed my arms under my breasts and peered out of the window. "That's tough. I might not like an artist's overall work, but one of their works might touch me or impress me with its technicality or emotion."

"You're stalling." He leaned forward and put his forearms on the table.

"I am not." My tone wasn't petulant, it was a bit high pitched, incredulous. With a huff, I clenched my arms a little tighter. "Fine. There's an artist out of Minneapolis named Melissa Cooke. She does these amazing hyper-realistic graphite and brush self-portraits. Some are quirky, some are strange. It's her ability to make her artwork so life-like is amazing. I also like Alfred Conteh and Amy Sherald, even though their art is very different than mine."

He nodded and clasped his hands, his long fingers wrapping around the backs. I don't know why they caught my attention. I couldn't help but watch the way they moved as well as their strength.

"I'll have to look them up," he said. "Does Harper share any of your talent?"

"Who said I have talent?"

"You don't go to art school without being able to draw more than a stick figure."

I unrolled my silverware and put my napkin in my lap, smoothing it more than once. "Maybe I draw the best stick figures ever."

He lightly kicked my shoe under the table. "You'll have to show me those sometime. I'd love to see them."

The rest of the meal was nice. We chatted about work and our experiences. The only problem was my body hummed like a tuning fork on overdrive the entire time we were together. What was it about Elliot that made my body stand up and shiver? Yes, he was attractive. He had these amazing chestnut curls that I'd never seen neat and tidy. They were always adorably tousled. His hazel eyes stood out from his lightly tanned skin, and when I was lucky, he wore a slight scruff that boosted his appeal even further.

I'd occasionally seen him in workout gear at the gym. I still don't know how I kept my tongue in my mouth instead of letting it loll around on the floor in front of me. It's a wonder I didn't fall flat on my face.

Yes, he was good-looking—no, he was fucking hot—and I knew other good-looking men who didn't affect me in the same way. Jensen, Charlie's husband, was known for the way he filled out a police uniform, yet I didn't have this reaction to him. Jena's fiancé, Brandon was attractive. Again, nothing when I'd first checked him out. I had no reaction to Ellie's husband either. Of course, that was a relief. The last thing I needed was to lust after one of my bosses' significant others!

After we paid the bill, we walked outside, more strolling than moving with a purpose.

"Can I ask you a question?" He watched his feet while we headed back in the direction of the hospital.

"You've already asked me several without permission."

His inhale was audible and uneven as he laughed under his breath. "Touché. I was just wondering about your parents."

I shoved my hands into the pockets of my jeans. "Where are yours?"

"Mine live in Louisiana. My dad still works part-time at Home Depot to help pay bills, and he's a handyman of sorts. Mom works for a florist."

"Is that where you grew up? In Louisiana?"

"I did," he said with a dip of his chin. "In Covington, which is across Lake Ponchartrain from New Orleans."

I watched one foot step in front of the other. "My mother died of cancer when I was three. My dad tried to go on. I believe he didn't know how to cope without her. He was in a car wreck a year later. He hit a tree off Highway 78. Thing is, no one knows why he was out that way. He had no reason to be." I'd never said the word suicide. The last thing I wanted to do was say it now.

"Gram took me in, raised me. She was great. She went to every school event and art exhibition. Now she takes care of Harper when I have to work. She sews and quilts, and even has her own Etsy shop. Most of her sales are quilts for cribs, bumper pads, and matching patchwork and crochet animals. Larger quilts take up a large amount of time, are expensive, and don't sell as often."

"Not much of a profit if you've spent a ton of time on it."

"That's why they're expensive."

As we approached the rotating front door, Elliot stopped and turned toward me. "I'm not going to barge into your grandmother's room while she's not feeling her best. Tell her I hope she feels better. I'll be by to check on her soon."

"Okay. Thank you for lunch."

I stared as his hand reached out and took mine, this odd current traveling up each and every nerve, creating this prickling that made me struggle not to squirm. "Do you need someone to pick up Harper?"

"Um, no, thanks. Jensen's picking her up and bringing her to his and Charlie's."

He nodded and tilted his head in the direction of the parking lot, letting it sort of pull him that way. "I should go." He held up a hand.

"Bye."

"Bye," I said. Shit, this was awkward!

When I went upstairs, Gram was sleeping, so I settled in and opened the reading app on my phone. I needed to get my mind off the way Elliot made me feel. Usually sappy romance novels were the perfect distraction when I needed one—except now, the handsome earl out to win his fair lady bore Elliot's face. Well, crap!

Chapter 3

On a sunny Saturday afternoon, I pulled up in front of Charlie and Jensen's house and shifted my car into park. The old brick mansion with the Mansard roof had belonged to Jensen's grandfather once upon a time, and Jensen had been restoring it for nearly a year now. A great deal had been renovated, but they weren't quite finished yet. He'd done considerably more to the outside since I'd last visited. Bright white trim on the windows now shone in the sun and the surrounding lawn was mowed and tidy. From what Charlie had said at work, the couple's latest projects hadn't been completing a study or dining room. Instead, they'd been remodeling a room for their baby, who was expected in early October.

I knocked on the front door and waited until Charlie cried out that she was on her way. Charlie was not a short woman, by any means, but she'd taken to waddling in the last month, which slowed her down considerably. When the door opened, she waved me inside. "Come on in. You have perfect timing. We just finished baking cookies."

Harper came running with her arms outstretched. "Mommy!"

I swung her up and back down so her feet landed on the floor. "Hey there, Sweet Pea. Did you have fun with Aunt Charlie?"

My daughter's head enthusiastically bobbed up and down as Charlie put her hands on Harper's shoulders. "Come on. Let's get some milk so you can have a cookie before you leave."

Harper climbed into a chair at the table and waited while Charlie slowly moved around the kitchen, fetching a small glass of milk and one of the ooey-gooey chocolate chip cookies.

"Thank you," said my daughter with this dreamy look in her eye. She was truly my daughter in that regard. There wasn't a chocolate we didn't like.

Charlie grinned and pulled herself onto a barstool with a sigh while we watched Harper eat. Charlie rubbed her big belly in large, circular motions. "How's your grandmother?"

"Annoyed that she can't do everything at once. Thank you for helping with Harper. I don't know how I would've managed today without you and Jensen."

"Maggie," she said, turning me around by my upper arms. "We've always invited you to parties and insisted you could bring Harper to the office if you needed it. You've never taken us up on any of our offers."

"You're my bosses."

"And hopefully your friends." Her hands squeezed my shoulders. "I know you have your grandmother, but no one can do everything on their own. It's laudable to try, but unrealistic."

I glanced over to Harper, who still ate while she chatted with the plush Stitch she'd propped on the table. "I don't want to take advantage either."

Charlie rolled her eyes and relaxed back into her seat. "Oh, please! How many times have you taken care of Freya to help out Ellie. You've fed Bacon when Jena and Brandon haven't taken her to Beaufort, and since I've been having problems with sciatica, you've picked up my slack at the office.

Let us help you too. I promise to let you know if you become an annoying bitch."

I spluttered out a laugh. "Good to know."

"You know what. I'll get you a glass of wine, we can have dinner, Harper can load up on cookies and watch Lilo and Stitch for probably the ten millionth time, and we can talk."

"I have to be able to drive home."

"Jensen!" called Charlie at the top of her lungs. After a moment and nothing, she yelled again.

Loud footsteps echoed through the house followed by running down the stairs. When he skidded to a halt in the doorway, his eyes were wide. "Is it time?"

"No, I'm hungry."

He pinched the bridge of his nose and exhaled heavily. "Woman, you're going to kill me one day."

She held up her swollen, bare feet. "I'm sorry if I scared you. I didn't want to get up to pour Maggie a glass of wine."

"I need to drive, Charlie," I repeated.

Jensen grabbed a bottle from a built-in rack and pulled a corkscrew from a drawer. "I can get one of the men on duty tonight to take you home. Granger even has a rookie, who could follow in your car."

"You don't have a wedding tomorrow." Charlie wore that expression that said she wouldn't be giving up until I agreed. "The entire office has the weekend off for Labor Day. That doesn't happen often, so we should take advantage. I could always call Jena and Ellie, and we could have a girls night in."

"I really can't stay all evening. Harper and I are going to church before we bring Gram lunch at the rehab facility."

She sighed with a shrug. "Have it your way."

Jensen set a glass of red in front of me. "I hope Malbec is okay. We haven't been keeping much wine around the house."

"It's fine, thanks."

He kissed Charlie quickly on the lips. "What do you want for dinner?"

She glanced up at the ceiling with an impish smile. "Oh, some salt and pepper squid, General Tso's chicken, spare ribs, and egg rolls."

"Is that it?" he asked while laughing. His hand rested splayed across her belly. When he looked at Charlie, his eyes were soft and adoring, and she had this air of contentedness she hadn't possessed before. I was so happy the two of them had worked through their past so they could have a future together.

She covered his hand with her own. "I wouldn't mind some crab Rangoon and lo mein, but I can do without them."

I bit my bottom lip while I tried to keep myself from bursting into giggles. I remembered those days. I also remembered how that bottomless pit sensation happened less and less toward the end of the pregnancy.

"Would you like anything, Maggie?" asked Charlie.

"Egg rolls and shrimp lo mein are good for me. If it's Chubby Panda, please tell them it's for Harper. They'll make sure she can eat it."

"That's great," said Charlie. "I didn't know they would do that."

"Harper has been friends with the owner's daughter since Head Start. They've always been amazing in ensuring it's not contaminated." Mei was probably the only mom friend I had from school. We weren't terribly close, but our daughters adored one another, and we always helped out the other if possible.

"If it's easier, I can order a pizza from the place next door to Chubby Panda." Jensen pulled his cell phone from his pocket and held it ready to dial.

"It's fine. After Mei insisted it was no problem to accommodate a peanut allergy, we order dinner from there about once every two weeks. Harper loves it." I took a sip of my wine, letting the rich flavor wash over my tongue.

"How's the wine?" asked Charlie. "Be detailed. I'm living vicariously through you."

I laughed and pulled up another barstool. "Didn't the doctor tell you that you could have a small glass on occasion?" I held out mine. "You can have a sip."

She shook her head. "No, it's too tempting to want to finish the entire glass. I so miss having wine with dinner—not that we drank every night."

I nodded and relaxed. "I know what you mean, even if I was underage when I found out I was pregnant."

"You never had a Turning twenty-one bash?" Jensen put a glass of something on the bar by Charlie, touched the screen on his phone, and put it to his ear as he left the room. "He's so sweet," said Charlie with a dramatic voice. "He makes me non-alcoholic cocktails that he keeps in the fridge. This one is honey, blackberry, and mint." One side of her lip curved wickedly. "Hardy har har, want to watch Stitch has a Glitch?"

My daughter cheered, jumped up, and grabbed her Stitch. Meanwhile, Charlie used the remote on the counter to turn on the television in the next room and stream the movie. Once Harper was settled on the sofa, Charlie turned back to me.

"When I start drinking again, we're all going out and having a belated twenty-first birthday celebration."

I held up and waved my hands. "That's really not necessary. Going out and getting wasted for the thrill of it holds very little appeal at this point."

"I can definitely understand. I think we all get to that point after a while." She took a sip of her drink and jumped with a "Mmm!" Her glass hit the countertop as she swallowed. "We should fix you up! When was the last time you went on a date?"

"No, no, no. I don't need a man in my life to be happy. I'm fine the way things are."

She shifted and pressed her hand against the side of her stomach. "Is Sawyer the reason you haven't dated in as long as I can remember?"

My head shot up. "God, no! I mean he hurt me when he left. I'm not still pining over him if that's what you mean. As far as I'm concerned, I got to keep the best part of him. The rest isn't worth a shit."

"Amen," said Charlie, holding up her glass.

I clinked my glass to hers. "It's simply that I can't imagine splitting my time any more than I already do. I also made a vow when Harper was born not to serial date. I won't bring a string of men into Harper's life only for them to leave without explanation."

"What if you found Mr. Right?" Charlie took the wine from my hands. "Couldn't she use a dad in her life?"

Could Harper use a dad? Sure, I suppose, but she wasn't an unhappy child. Why stir up something that hadn't posed a problem? "Why are you doing this?"

34

"Because you can't be alone for the rest of your life."

I took my glass back and frowned. "I never said I'd be alone forever."

"Good! Remember that I was celibate from the time Jensen and I broke up until we got back together. Trust me, more than a decade of self-imposed celibacy is not fun. Every woman needs a sex life."

"Mommy, what's a sex life?"

The modern, long-stemmed wine goblet nearly slipped from my hand. "Just a boring adult thing. Is something wrong?"

Harper tilted her head and looked back and forth between me and Charlie. I knew that look. I'd seen it on Harper's face dozens of times. She wasn't buying it. "Can I have some water, please?"

"Sure." Charlie waddled around the island to give her a glass. Harper took one tiny sip before running back into the living room.

"Sorry," said Charlie, her cheeks pink.

"Let's hope she doesn't ask Gram. Knowing my grandmother, she'd explain everything to her in vivid detail. Lord knows she did when I asked."

Charlie climbed back onto her barstool chuckling. "I love that woman. I want to be her when I grow up—minus the quilting. I'd go batshit crazy in a matter of a few hours if I had to sew."

We both sat silent for a moment. I sipped my wine and glanced over to Harper, who giggled at one of Stitch's antics in the movie. I loved that sound. It was the best thing in the world. I swallowed and stared into my glass. "There is someone I'm attracted to."

"Really?" Charlie's eyes were huge as they danced. "Who?" She leaned forward so she was a hair closer and rested an arm on the counter. Her hand kept massaging her bump. "I know it's none of my business, so whatever you tell me won't go any further—well, other than Jensen of course, but I promise he's as tight-lipped as they come."

A high-pitched laugh escaped before I could stop it. "No, sorry. I don't need you riding my ass to give the guy a chance."

Charlie sat up straighter and pressed a palm to her chest. "Me?" She sagged back to her former position. "Okay, I totally would. I only want everyone to be as happy as I am."

"I get it, and I appreciate it. I'm just not sure about letting someone into our lives. The bad thing is that I'm sure Gram suspects and will start playing matchmaker as soon as she comes home."

"A woman after my own heart," said Charlie.

I took another sip of my wine while I considered the best way to protect myself without offending Elliot in the process. The last thing I needed was for Charlie to discover the man I had the hots for was one of her best friends. I'd never stand a chance!

After my glass of wine, I'd somehow managed to convince Charlie that I didn't need a second, so I was good to drive home after dinner. I pulled the car into the garage and opened the door for Harper. We'd barely stepped into the backyard, when I halted in my tracks. What in the holy heck?

"Hey!" Elliot straightened, his long legs unfolding until he stood at his full six-foot something height. He was next to the deck off the screened-in porch, wearing a pair of well-worn cargo shorts and a Red Hot Chili Peppers t-shirt that clung to his pecs in the best possible way. An armband tattoo I'd only ever seen glimpses of peeked from one sleeve. I so wanted to rip that shirt from him to see exactly what was underneath.

I shook myself from the fantasy to the garden hose that lay on the ground with a bag of quick-dry concrete and a post that emerged in a straight line from the dirt. That post hadn't been there before.

"What are you doing?" I took a few steps forward. Some lumber was next to the steps along with another couple of bags of the concrete.

"Your grandmother will be home in a few days so I wanted to help you out by getting those steps fixed and installing a ramp in the event she needs it." He scratched the back of his neck.

"The doctor expects to discharge her on Tuesday. She's walking, but they wanted to make sure she's steady enough not to fall again."

"That's good."

I pointed to the lumber. "I have steps stained and ready to be installed. I simply hadn't had the time to do it, and when I did have the time, the weather worked against me."

With a hand to Harper's shoulder, I pressed her forward. "Harper, this is Mr. Elliot. He was one of the EMTs who helped Gram on Wednesday."

"Hi," she said softly before skipping over to Gram's roses. She and Gram always sniffed the blooms together.

I smiled and shook my head. "She's so outgoing with me and those she knows, I forget how shy she can be with others."

"It's okay. I wouldn't want you to push her."

"So, about those steps. I appreciate you helping, but I can manage."

"We're friends, right?" He stood straight and tall, the dust from the concrete clinging to his dark shirt. The places where the shirt stuck to his abdomen from sweat made the dust more noticeable. Why did a man doing manual labor always kick-start a woman's hormones?

"Sure," I said hesitantly.

"So, friends help one another out. You have to admit it's better to have this done before your grandmother comes home. Otherwise, when would you have the time?"

As much as I hated to admit it, he had a point. "You're right. I apologize if I was rude. I appreciate the help."

"No worries." He picked up the bag of cement and shifted it away. "I've got the supports in for the ramp. If you have those steps, I'll get them installed."

"Harper, I'll unlock the door if you want to go inside. You can color or get out the clay."

"Can I paint?"

"Not right now." I wasn't in the mood to scrub a ton of tempera paint off the table.

I lifted Harper to the deck, and after letting her into the house, I pulled the pre-measured steps from behind the rattan love seat. I'd kept them in the screened-in porch since I'd stained them a month ago.

Elliot took them from me carefully and carried them outside. "These are great, but we still might have a problem."

"What do you mean?"

He took a crowbar and pulled the weathered wood away from the frame while I watched his arms flex and relax. Little bits of his armband peeked further from the sleeve yet never quite giving away what it was.

After he set aside the tool, he pointed to what was underneath. "If you could screw those planks into place without cracking the framing, replacing the top of the steps would be a temporary fix. The underside is rotting as well."

"Crap," I muttered. I hadn't even considered that as a possibility.

"Look, I have enough wood to make up for what we need. Next weekend, I thought we could put up a railing. "

I brushed back my hair from my face. The humidity was making my curls a frizzy mess. "First, I'm paying you back for everything you've bought. Second, give me a chance to change clothes so I can help you."

A wide grin split his face, making two distinct dimples appear like magic on his cheeks. Argh! My breath always caught in my lungs when those dimples made an appearance. "I certainly won't turn down your help."

I climbed onto the deck. "Great, I'll be back soon."

As I walked into the house, the tell-tale sound of him taking apart what remained of the steps followed me. The last thing I needed was to spend the evening with a sweaty, sexy Elliot Martin. Sighing, I climbed the stairs toward my bedroom. Did I own something that would repulse him?

In the end, I found an old, ratty pair of jean cut-offs and a shirt I'd used when I'd painted my bedroom two years ago. It was too hot for sweats, so I had to hope he would consider this unappealing? After one glance at myself in the mirror, I made my way downstairs. I was on a mission—to get rid of this attraction once and for all. Problem was I didn't know if I was trying to get rid of mine or his!

Chapter 4

I'd just opened my closet on Saturday morning when a sound downstairs made me step back and be as quiet as I could manage. Was that sound what I thought it was? The knock repeated itself as Gram called me from her perch on the sofa. I hurried down the stairs to the front door, wrapping my robe around myself before I glanced through the peephole.

I drew back with a jerk. What was he doing here, and so early on a Saturday?

"Who is it?" asked Gram.

When I opened the door, Elliot smiled and held out a cup of coffee. "Good morning."

My hand wrapped around the warm cup from Starlight and pulled it closer. "Thanks," I said slowly. "Did I forget something?"

I'd seen Elliot at the gym twice this week and once at the grocery store. We always talked whenever we bumped into one another. Of course, some days we chatted more than others. Lately, he asked about Gram and Harper, and I'd made sure I'd asked if his license had come through. Nothing was mentioned about dropping by on Saturday morning.

"We'd discussed finishing up the stairs this weekend. I didn't consider that you might have plans." His eyes traced over my face. "Based on your hair and make-up, I'd guess something special."

My hand flew to my hair, which Gram had managed to tame and pull back into a braided up-do. "Jena's wedding is today. I assumed you were going?"

He shrugged and leaned against the door frame. "I've met her, of course, but I don't know her very well."

Gram called over from her comfortable sofa corner. "Margaret, where are your manners? Invite the young man inside."

I stepped back from the door as Elliot peered around me. "Good morning, Mrs. Dashwood."

"Oh, call me Cora." Gram's eyelashes practically batted as she smiled. I barely kept myself from rolling my eyes.

"Yes, ma'am," he said as I motioned for him step across the threshold. "How are you feeling, Mrs. Dashwood?"

"I'd be much better if Maggie would let me do something around this house. Do you know she won't even let me load the dishwasher? I can walk well with the walker, but she still won't hear of it."

He nodded and stepped over to Gram while I closed the door. "I'm sure you're capable, but you'll heal more fully if you don't resume all of your usual activities right away."

This time, Gram rolled her eyes and huffed. Elliot's shoulders shook while his smile grew wider. "How are your physical therapy exercises going?"

"She hasn't been doing them," said Harper from the kitchen table. "My mommy was fussing at her for it yesterday."

My grandmother crossed her arms over her chest and gave Harper a stern glare over her glasses. "Thank you for that." She turned back to Elliot. "I'd like them better if they didn't make me sore."

He sat across from her and propped his elbows on his knees. "Those exercises are meant to strengthen your hip so you don't injure it again. Am I going to have to come by and make sure you're following doctor's orders?"

Gram's eyes made this slight shift to me. Oh, crap! That woman would love nothing more than to have a handsome man helping with her physical therapy several times a week. I also suspected that she'd use this in an effort to set me up with a man she happens to like. She'd never liked Sawyer, even before we broke up, though she'd never said why.

I gulped hard as he stood from the sofa and my eyes honed in on his toned rear end. I was in big trouble. If my grandmother agreed to his help with her physical therapy, and he wore shorts like he was wearing today, I might have to take a huge bite out of his ass.

"Sweetheart," said Gram with a wide-eyed smile. That look was one worthy of convincing a priest she'd never sinned in her life. I knew better.

"Yes, Gram?"

"Maybe Elliot could go with you to the wedding."

Why did I suddenly feel like Samantha in Sixteen Candles when her grandparents insisted she take Long Duck Dong to the dance? "He may not want to go. Besides, I'm not simply a guest. I'm also coordinating everything."

"I know, but wouldn't it be nice to have company for the reception?"

"It's okay, Cora," said Elliot with a smile. "I think Maggie would rather go on her own." He lightly rested that fine ass on the back of my sofa while he spoke to me. "What about Harper and your grandmother? Do you have someone coming over for them?"

I crossed my arms over my chest, even though I still held my coffee in my hand. "Gram and Harper will be fine. Mei and her daughter Lu, who's Harper's best friend, are coming over around lunchtime to bring them food. Mei said they'd stay for an hour or two so the girls can play."

"Well, if it's okay, I'll work on the steps and the ramp. That concrete should be good and cured by now."

I sagged back against the door. I couldn't have him doing manual labor around the house without my help. Just the thought of leaving him here to work made me feel guilty. "Would you like to go to the wedding with me?"

"You don't have to take me. I'm a big boy, you know." One side of his lips curved up in this wicked grin. Damn if he wasn't flirting with me. I certainly hadn't needed him to point that fact out to me. I'd known he was a full-grown man for a while now.

"I know that. It's one thing for you to help me with fixing the deck, but I'm not going to leave you to do it on your own. You aren't slave labor."

He glanced at his watch. "What time do you have to be at the wedding?"

I stepped around so I could see Gram's antique clock on the shelf. "Shit! Twenty minutes."

"Mommy, you have to put a dollar in the swear jar!"

As I shook my head, I pointed at Harper. "I'll do it when I get home. I have to get dressed and go."

Before Gram could say a word, I ran up the stairs two at a time and threw on my cornflower blue wrap dress with white flowers. I loved the flowy skirt which worked perfectly for my height when I wore my platform sandals.

I grabbed my purse and booked it downstairs where I slipped on my heels and grabbed my gift from the kitchen table. When I turned, Elliot sat on the sofa, near Gram, sipping his coffee.

"Don't worry about us, dear," said Gram with a sly grin. "We'll be here when you get back."

I pointed at Elliot and levelled my sternest glare. "Don't work on the deck without me." He merely waved me off as I closed the porch door behind me.

⁂

Three hours later, I stood on the pavers that made up the patio behind the office. We'd done a lot to the spacious yard in the past few years, adding a gazebo in one corner as well as more potted plants and flower beds. We didn't have clients use the space often, but it was a great spot for small weddings and receptions when the rare occasion presented itself.

The ceremony had been beautiful. Jena glowed in her ivory satin gown, and Freya, Jena's niece and Ellie's daughter, stared at her aunt as though she were a fairy princess.

While I stood to one side with a glass of champagne, Charlie stepped up beside me, rubbing her belly as she did almost constantly these days. "Look at my brother," she said, flicking her chin in Brandon's direction. "He hasn't stopped grinning since he woke up this morning. If his mouth keeps stretching, it's going to crack his face in two."

We both giggled while Brandon remained oblivious, twirling his new wife out and back in for a dip. "He's happy. They both are. At least they're old enough to know exactly what they want and who makes them happy."

Charlie's arm looped through mine. "I don't think it's a matter of age. I knew I wanted Jensen, and he knew he wanted me when we were sixteen. We simply had a difference of opinion as to when that was supposed to occur."

I took a sip of my champagne and swallowed while I watched the bride and groom continue to dance and kiss in the middle of the make-shift dance floor.

"Do you think you and Sawyer were too young?"

"I suppose I wasn't," I said. "I just didn't realize he was. I thought he would be there for whatever was thrown our way."

"You've never told me why you broke up." Charlie's voice was soft. "I think everyone simply assumed it was because of Harper."

"More because I wouldn't put her up for adoption. After he signed away his rights, he did his best to convince me to do the same."

"You've said enough for me to know you don't regret it," said Charlie. "You're an amazing mother. You work your ass off for her to have whatever she needs. I admire you for it."

My eyes burned and watered. I wasn't going to cry! "Thanks."

Charlie's finger on her free hand pointed at me. "Don't you dare start blubbering because I'll join you before the first tear hits your chin." Her hand wrapped around to her back and rubbed some more. "Damn if these Braxton-Hicks aren't killing me today." She blew out a heavy breath as I shifted around to face her.

"Are you sure they're false labor?"

"I'm still three weeks away from my due date," she gritted out through her teeth. "It's just with the back pain I've had for the last month, Braxton-Hicks make me miserable."

I set down my glass on a nearby table. "Humor me and let's time them."

"It's not labor, Maggie."

"Like I said, humor me." After I steered her to a nearby chair, I pulled up another, facing her, and opened the stopwatch on my phone. "Let me know when the next one starts."

After watching the happy couple for a time, Charlie gripped my free hand. "Mother trucker," she said, squeezing as though she were trying with all of her strength to amputate my fingers. I touched "start" on my phone but it was the clock that concerned me. It'd only been three minutes since I unlocked my phone.

Her grip let up, and she relaxed when it ended. "I'm so tired. I can't wait to have him and hold him in my arms instead of him pressing on my sciatic nerve."

"He'll be here sooner than you think. I promise. If we didn't have the swollen feet and uncomfortable parts to make us crazy, we'd want to stay pregnant forever."

My eyes met Jensen's. He'd been talking to William, Ellie's husband, by the bar for a while, though he'd stopped paying attention to William. His forehead furrowed. "Is she okay?" he mouthed.

I shrugged as best I could without Charlie seeing. She'd raise hell if I scared Jensen out of his wits. Right as I turned back to her, she gripped my hand again. I may not have had a perfect time from earlier, but it gave me a close enough time to compare.

As Charlie let up four contractions later, Jensen appeared at her side. "What's up, buttercup?"

"Dear, Lord," she said breathlessly. "How much have you had to drink?"

He laughed and kissed her hair. "One glass of champagne. I promise." She leaned her head back and closed her eyes, and Jensen lifted his eyebrows in my direction. I'd been using the stopwatch and hitting lap for each contraction, so it listed the times for each gap. He took a deep breath when he saw them, but fortunately, it wasn't loud.

"How's our little slugger?" He sat in the chair beside her and flattened his hand against her stomach. When she gripped my hand again, he kissed her temple. "Breathe, Charlie."

"I'm not in labor."

"Your last four contractions have been exactly four minutes apart, and your stomach is hard as a rock. We're going to the hospital."

"It's a wasted trip. I don't want to miss Jena and Brandon leaving," she whined.

After approximately five minutes of coaxing and another pain, we finally managed to get Charlie's grumbling surrender, but when Jensen helped her stand, she nearly crumpled in front of him.

"Fuckity-fuck-fuck," she muttered.

Jensen whispered in her ear while she breathed heavily and leaned against him. "Don't forget that you aren't supposed to use that word anymore, Mrs. Worth."

"Shut the fuck up." She managed to pant out between breaths.

When the pain subsided, she lifted the bottom of her maxi-dress where a small puddle was now soaking into the stone pavers. "My water broke."

The next five minutes were a flurry of excitement as Jensen hustled Charlie toward their car while I informed Jena and Brandon as well as the Taylors, Charlie and Brandon's parents. Jena and Brandon departed not long after, and the rest of the reception didn't take long to follow.

Greta and I hauled all of the gifts upstairs to Jena and Brandon's home, which was above our office in that historic brick house. We also locked up once the caterers finished cleaning and the rental company had loaded the tables and chairs.

As soon as I arrived home, I kicked off my shoes and dropped back against the door. "You look exhausted—beautiful but exhausted."

My eyes shot open to Elliot sitting on the sofa watching Disney channel with Harper, who was more interested in the television than who walked through the door. "Where's Gram?"

"She's taking a nap. Working on her physical therapy tired her out."

"Thanks for helping with that."

"It's no bother. She does like flirting, which is something I should get used to with some ladies."

"Oh, Lord," I sighed. "I'm almost afraid to ask."

"Nothing bad. Just some blushing and batting her eyelashes."

I blew out a loud exhale and stepped into the room, dropping into the sage-colored arm chair. "Well, it definitely could've been worse."

"How was the wedding?"

"Beautiful, except the reception wrapped up a bit early because Charlie went into labor."

He sat forward and turned more to face me. "Are you serious?"

"As a quadruple bypass. She insisted it was Braxton-Hicks until her water broke."

With a snicker, he leaned back again. "With that hard head of hers, I'm not surprised. Still, isn't it a somewhat early?"

"She has three more weeks until her due date. From what I remember, the lungs should be developed by thirty-seven weeks. He should be okay."

"Good," he said. "She's a good friend. I want to see her and Jensen happy. They deserve it."

"Yes, they do. Mrs. Taylor said she'd call when there was news. I think the entire family followed Charlie and Jensen to the hospital." I brushed a few curls back from my face. No matter how we pulled it back, my hair always did have a mind of its own.

"Have you eaten?"

I propped an elbow on the side of the chair and supported my head. "I ate a little at the reception before the caterer needed me for something. By the time I'd returned, my plate had been picked up."

"Your friend Mei left food for you when she came."

"But then I'd have to get up," I said with a weak chuckle.

Elliot stood and stepped around the sofa. "If you want, I can heat it up for you while you change."

I laid my head on the back of the chair as he walked toward the kitchen. "You would do that?"

"Of course." He walked back and held out his hands. "Come on. Up! Before you fall asleep in your dress."

My hands tingled like they'd been asleep when his fingers closed around them. After he helped haul my butt out of the chair, I caught his eye. "Just out of curiosity. Why are you still here?"

"Your grandmother kept insisting I stay. I also thought having someone here in the event your grandmother fell again wouldn't be such a bad idea."

"They wouldn't have been alone for long."

His one shoulder shrugged as he looked down to our hands where they were still joined between us. "I know, and I'm sure they would've been fine. I simply didn't want to take any chances."

"That's sweet."

"No, no, no." He groaned and shook his head. "A grown man isn't sweet or cute. He's ruggedly handsome or hot as hell. Sweet is the kiss of death."

I rolled my eyes before I rose on my tiptoes and planted a kiss to his cheek. "I happen to like sweet," I whispered near his ear.

His eyebrows were nearly in his hairline when I pulled back, but I waited until I turned away and was climbing the stairs before I smiled. If only Elliot knew some of the dialogue that rattled around my brain, he might not have been so disappointed in "sweet."

Chapter 5

My eyes popped open as my body jolted. I lifted my head and scanned the room. When had I gone to bed? Elliot had a plate of Chinese vegetables and an egg roll ready and waiting for me after I'd changed. He sat and talked to me while I ate. Then, we sat down in front of the TV, and I didn't remember anything more. How early had I fallen asleep?

I dragged myself out of bed and pulled on my cut-offs with a t-shirt. After I brushed my teeth and quickly braided my hair, I hurried downstairs and started a pot of coffee.

At a soft knock, I hurried to let Elliot inside. He'd wanted to get an early start so we would be finished before the hottest part of the day. "Morning," he said with a soft smile.

"Morning. I've got coffee going. Do you want some?"

"Sure, thanks." He sat at the island that we used more as a table than a workspace. "Do you mind if I eat something before we start? I just woke up."

"Of course, not."

I set a mug in front of him and filled it. Before I could put milk and sugar in front of him, he took a big sip. "Did you want these?" I held up the sugar bowl and the milk carton.

"No, thanks. I'll take it as it is. It's good."

"Thanks. Do you want breakfast? Harper and Gram will be up any minute. They're always early risers."

"Oh," he said as he dug something out of his shorts pocket. "I brought a protein bar."

My eyes latched onto the words "peanut butter" on the wrapper. "Harper is severely allergic to peanuts, so if you want to eat it, you'll need to go out in the yard and throw the wrapper in the garbage cans outside. Gram and I keep the house peanut free so Harper is as safe as possible."

"Let me put this in the bag on my bike. I'd rather not take a chance." He ran out of the front door and returned a moment later. "Your friend brought Chinese food yesterday. I would think that would be nearly impossible."

I started pulling out ingredients for pancakes. "Mei is amazing. When we order food, she always makes it herself. I'm really thankful for her since otherwise we'd rarely ever be able to eat out, and Harper loves it."

He took a gulp of his coffee and slid between the island and the counter. "How can I help?"

"You can take out the syrup and put some plates next to the stove." I glanced up to the cupboard in front of me.

As I cracked an egg into the batter, he shifted behind me and opened the glass-fronted cabinet that held the plates. His chest rubbed against my back, giving me a full feel of his defined pecs. He set four dishes on the counter then paused. "Are you okay?"

"Of course, why?"

"Because you haven't moved since I stepped behind you." His voice held a certain quality that I'd only heard when he was amused. "Are those goosebumps?"

A finger trailed along that sensitive point where my neck met my shoulder, and I swallowed a gasp. "Elliot." His name was all raspy and pathetic, but that ever so slight touch made my skin prickle as I shivered.

When his lips brushed against my shoulder, I leaned more into the cabinets to keep myself standing. His hand cupped my cheek and gently turned my head so our eyes met, and he dipped down to press his lips against mine.

This strangled groan erupted from my chest as I turned and lunged for more. I couldn't tell you who opened their mouth first, but at the first touch of our tongues, I melted into him. His hands landed on my hips and drew me closer until my breasts were crushed against his chest, and my fingers dug into his biceps as I anchored myself to keep from dissolving into a puddle at his feet.

"Mommy?"

Harper may as well have doused us with a bucket of ice water. I hurtled away from him and turned back to the counter. "Morning, Sweet Pea."

"Hey, Harpoon," said Elliot. "I hope you're hungry. Your mommy's making pancakes."

She giggled as she sat in the chair Elliot vacated earlier. "Harpoon?"

After I cracked the last egg, he took the whisk from the countertop. "Here let me do that while you get the griddle ready."

My cheeks burned like they were a four-alarm fire as I shifted over to the stove and switched it on. Just great, Maggie. One moment of temptation and you threw yourself at him. Only your daughter walked in to witness you playing the part of wanton whore.

"Can I have blueberries in mine?"

"Great idea," said Elliot. "What do you think, Mommy?"

"She's not your mommy," giggled Harper.

When he placed the bowl beside me, I ladled six small pancakes onto the griddle and pulled the blueberries from the refrigerator, placing them precisely into the pancakes. Elliot chuckled from beside me at the smiley face I'd made on two of them.

Once Harper was settled with her pancakes, we made our own and ate while I made some for Gram, who appeared right when they came off the griddle.

As much as I hated to admit it, I loved watching Elliot with Harper. He joked and laughed with her and asked her questions about school and her friends. Harper wasn't always the most outgoing, but she was no longer being shy with him.

"What's your least favorite part of P.E. so far?"

School had only started a couple of weeks ago, but she'd already told Gram and me how much she hated P.E. and why.

Harper's little face puckered. "Volleyball."

"What?" he exclaimed with a hand to his chest as if he was wounded. "How could you not like volleyball?"

She shrugged dramatically. "I don't get it. I never know when to swap places and how to hit the ball."

Elliot leaned onto the island so he was face to face with her. "I can help you with that, you know. So can Charlie when she's feeling up to it. She played volleyball in college and could've gone to the Olympics if she hadn't hurt herself."

"What are the 'lympics?"

Despite trying not to laugh, my shoulders shook. With a glance behind, he busted me pressing my lips together.

His eyes narrowed. "Why's that funny?"

"Because the last Olympics were when she was four, and the last summer Olympics was when she was two."

He lunged at me, and I shrieked as he dug his fingers into my ribs and tickled. "Didn't anyone ever teach you that it's not nice to laugh at someone?"

Next thing I knew, Harper had run around and joined him, her little talons digging much harder than Elliot's. "Ow! Okay, I give up."

Gram's smile was a mile wide while she ate. "The two of you better get outside if you want to finish before that heat settles in." I peered over at the clock. It was only seven-thirty, but as much as I hated to leave the air conditioning, Gram was right.

I opened the dishwasher, and Elliot joined me as we both put our dishes inside. When all that was left was the griddle, we made our way out to the back porch and pulled the supplies onto the deck. We'd already pre-cut all of the wood that Elliot was preparing to slide into place.

"By the way, how did I end up in bed last night? I remember coming downstairs and eating before you put on that old movie for Harper. Next thing I knew, I woke up this morning in my bed."

"I tried to wake you, but you mumbled and curled more into the chair. In the end, I carried you. Harper showed me which room was yours. Not that I couldn't have figured it out with the collection of Stitch toys Harper has in her window seat.

He put one end of the ramp support where he'd marked. "Come hold this for me."

I grabbed that side while Elliot used the power screwdriver to attach it to the posts. "Thanks for doing that— carrying me, I mean."

"You don't need to thank me," he said, grinning. He grabbed another screw and lined it up with the power tool. "You're downright chatty when you're sleeping. Carrying you to bed was the highlight of my day."

"What did I say?" With both ends of the beam attached, I let go and put my hands on my hips at Elliot's mischievous grin. "Seriously, Elliot, tell me."

After he put in another screw, he stood. "Tell you what. Kiss me again like you did in the kitchen, and I'll consider it."

"Ha!" burst from my mouth, and I pushed past him to the supplies. "You're evil."

"Nah, it was simply the best kiss I've ever had, and I want you to do it again."

"So, what? I wasn't talking in my sleep?"

He laughed while he bent down to continue working. "I didn't say that."

At a chirp from my phone, I opened my messages app. "That's from Mrs. Taylor. Charlie had a boy at about one in the morning. She lists his weight and length. Oh! She sent a picture." I covered my mouth with my palm while I laughed. "He looks like Charlie."

Elliot stepped behind me and looked over my shoulder, snickering. In the photo, the baby's face was screwed up like he was about to let out one impressive wail. "I'd recognize that pissed off expression anywhere. Charlie makes that same face when the opponent scores."

I elbowed him in the arm. "Be nice."

"Hey, I'm completely serious. Does this future Clemson volleyball player have a name?"

I minimized the photo. "Wyatt James Worth." I sent Mrs. Taylor a quick text thanking her and locked my phone.

The two of us set back to work, talking mostly about Charlie and the new baby. Once we had the second long beam installed, Elliot stood and stretched. "Do you ever want another?"

"Baby?"

"Well, yes. We weren't discussing gerbils."

"Ha, ha. I don't know. I suppose I never gave it much thought. I've been so caught up in making a life for me and Harper that I've never considered the future all that much—other than in a big picture sort of way: that Harper will grow up, go to college, and so on." I handed him the next piece of wood. "What about you?"

We both bent over so I could hold it while he attached it. "I wouldn't mind one or two."

After his answer, our conversation turned to less personal topics: whether I enjoyed sports, his favorite football team, what movies were our favorites, then the same with music. The ramp was finished rather quickly, and we put in the railings for the steps as well. Whichever method Gram preferred to go inside the house, she now possessed both.

"Do you want some water?" I asked after we'd gathered the tools.

"That'd be great. Do you mind if we put the tool box in the garage so I can pick them up later? It'll be difficult to tote them around on my bike."

"It's fine. I can always drop them by sometime, although I don't know where you live."

"I live on the river. Down that trail when you reach the end of the Riverwalk."

"I've seen the trail, but I've never been down that way."

"You should bring Harper sometime. I have a canoe and two kayaks, and you can fish from the deck."

"She'd love the kayaks and the canoe. I can't see her touching a worm or a fish."

After we'd put everything on a shelf near the garage door, he followed me back into the yard and into the porch. I opened the door to the kitchen, and the rich smell of tomato sauce and cheese flooded my nose, making my stomach growl. "Gram, are you cooking one of the lasagnas from the freezer?" I'd told Gram to stay out of the kitchen for now—not that she had to do much but remove the lid from the container and pop it in the oven.

"Harper was getting hungry. It should be ready soon."

"But that's not enough food for all of us."

Gram waved my comment away dismissively. "I thought you and your young man could go out when you were done. It would certainly be a nice way to thank him."

"Gram!"

"Yeah, Mommy," said Harper with a sassy tone. "You never go anywhere that's not work."

"Harper!"

Elliot's low laugh rumbled behind me. "I think you've been outmaneuvered."

I flashed my grandmother the meanest glare I could muster before I pulled the pitcher of water from the fridge and poured Elliot and me a glass. "I do appreciate the help. Sorry if I was moody about it."

His smile morphed into this adorable lopsided grin. "No worries. Why don't you get cleaned up so we can do as your grandmother suggested? I'll ride home, shower, dress, and return for you."

"Okay, I guess." I glanced over at Gram while I tried not to think about Elliot in the shower—naked in the shower. I mentally shook myself. "I suppose you'll need to decide what you want to eat."

"You do the same."

Before I could think about it, he kissed my cheek. "See you in a bit."

"Yeah," I managed before he high-tailed it through the door.

I walked over to the coffee table, picked up the remote, and paused the movie Gram was watching with Harper. "What was that?"

"I'm doing you a favor, dear. You're always so serious. He'd be good for you."

Harper turned around and shifted up to her knees so she sat higher. "He's fun, and if you marry him, we could hang out and play every day."

I shook my head. "You two are impossible." After pressing play, I headed upstairs. I couldn't believe Gram had Harper in on her scheme. That little development was the last thing I ever expected.

After a quick shower, I attempted to tame my corkscrew curls while I chanted in my head, "This is not a date. This is not a date." Who was I kidding? After that lip-lock I'd laid on him this morning, I'd be lucky to make it through this afternoon without shucking my panties!

With a groan, I opened my closet and stared. What did you wear for a non-date date? I didn't even know where we were going or what we were doing. I groaned. When her hip was fully healed, I was going to kill Gram.

I grabbed a black, lace-trimmed halter top and a flowy earth-tone skirt. Once I had my black sandals on, I ran back downstairs. Fidgety, I picked up a rag and wiped down the counters while Harper brought the dishes into the kitchen from lunch and loaded them in the dishwasher.

"Thank you," I said before she skipped out and upstairs.

"Gram, just because I'll be gone doesn't mean you can start playing 'Baby Got Back' and dancing around the living room. Take it easy."

My grandmother turned around with a smile that made me freeze in place. "For someone who claims not to like the boy, you sure are nervous."

"I'm not nervous."

"Harper said the two of you were kissing this morning." My grandmother sang it, making me want to knock her upside the head.

I closed my eyes. "That shouldn't have happened."

"Why?" When I opened my eyes, Gram's amusement had disappeared, replaced by slightly lifted eyebrows and a steady, penetrating gaze from those dark brown eyes that had years of wisdom behind them.

"I don't need a man. I'm fine with things the way they are. It would just be time away from Harper, and you, and possibly the office."

"Margaret, come here."

At the sound of my full name, issued in the same voice as when I was a child, my feet followed her command. As soon as my butt hit the sofa cushion, Gram took my hand. "I'm so proud of you. I know most of the time I rattle it off like it's no big deal, but never doubt how serious I am. You've busted your ass to make a life for yourself and Harper after that little weasel of a boy ditched you."

I couldn't help but give a slight laugh. "You never liked him."

"Damn right. He was a self-centered little douche in high school and that obviously didn't change in college. But as you'll learn with Harper, I couldn't tell you how to live your life. You loved him and swore you'd be together forever. If I'd told you my beliefs, you'd have ignored me and possibly cut me out of your life.

"That's beside the point, though. You finished your degree—maybe not the one you'd planned, but one that would put food on the table. You've worked your way up since you were hired by those three young women a few years ago. You've dedicated yourself to Harper and me for all of this time, but you need something for you too. You can't simply live for everyone but yourself. Everyone in this world needs to take care of themselves somehow—whether it's alone time shopping, or reading, or time with someone special."

"I get my alone time when I work out."

She shook her head and squeezed my hand. I stared at our joined hands, her darker hand weathered more than the one that soothed me as a little girl. "But every moment of your time other than that is spent working, cooking, cleaning, or taking care of Harper and me. You haven't dated since *that boy* left you. If you continue on, one day, you'll be my age. I'll be gone, Harper will be an adult with a life of her own—not that she'd exclude you, but she'll live with her husband and her own children. Who will you spend your time with? You could use a man, and frankly, Harper could use a father in her life."

"Gram—"

"I love you, dear. I can tell you're attracted to Elliot because you turn all sorts of interesting shades of red when he's around, and he likes you too. Those gorgeous eyes of his never leave you for very long. So, I want you to go to dinner with him, get to know him a bit better, and don't poke your head through that door until . . ." She looked at the clock. "It's three now. Don't set foot in that door before nine."

"Really, Gram."

"I'm serious. Harper and I will be fine. She's gathering art supplies to bring down. We're going to listen to music and color. Then we agreed to play a game or two before we put on another movie. I promise not to move unless I have to. I want you to promise me you'll give him a chance."

Harper bustled back in, dumping a bunch of paper, markers, and crayons on the table. A knock came from the door, and she peeked through the front window. "It's Elliot!" She ran over and opened the door as Gram gave my arm a slight pull and levelled that look that insisted I obey without question.

"Okay, Gram. I promise."

Chapter 6

As I closed the door behind me, Elliot turned and walked backwards slowly. "You look nice."

"Thanks. Do you have anywhere in particular you'd like to go?"

"I'd thought about Giuseppe's or Mugs."

"Italian or burgers. You're going all out, Martin."

He smiled and put out his hands in a sort of mock shrug. "Since you're the one taking me out, I thought I'd be a cheap date—not too cheap mind you."

I spluttered when I laughed. "I think I'd use the word inexpensive.

He turned and fell into step beside me. "I think I like cheap." He nudged my shoulder with his. "What do you think?"

"That either way, I'm going to have to kill myself at the gym tomorrow to make up for it."

His hand slipped around mine so easily I was almost uncomfortable. "We can work out together if you want."

Gram's house sat in a small alley, so when we reached Main street, we paused. If we wanted Mugs, we'd need to turn left. If we wanted Giuseppe's, we had to go right and head toward the Riverwalk. "You don't have a preference?" I asked.

His head leaned right as he pulled me toward the Riverwalk. "We can walk along the river after we eat. Hopefully, it'll have cooled down by then."

Gram and I didn't live too far from the river, so in a matter of minutes, we stepped off the road and down the pathway toward the row of quaint shops and restaurants. When we entered Giuseppe's, we were greeted by the owner, who seated us at one of the nicer tables by the window. As it was late for lunch and too early for dinner, only one other table sat on the opposite end of the dining room, which appeared to be Giuseppe's wife and children. I recognized his son from Harper's school.

Elliot ordered a beer, and I ordered a glass of red wine before Giuseppe left us to peruse the menus. "Do you have a favorite?" I asked. "We don't go out to eat very often. Harper's diet is easier to control at home."

He frowned while he continued to look at the menu. "I've never noticed nuts on the menu."

"If they have pesto, then there are pine nuts. Not as bad as a bakery or Thai food, but still a pain."

"I hadn't considered that one." He rested his menu on the table and looked up. "Do you want to share a pizza and a salad?"

"That depends." I set my menu down as well. "What are you thinking?"

"I was actually thinking Margherita."

"Simple and classic," I said. "We could have the arugula salad. I love Caprese, but that's a lot of tomato and mozzarella."

"You can never go wrong with tomatoes and mozzarella." His expression was so stone-cold serious, I snorted when I laughed.

I covered my nose while my cheeks warmed. "I can't believe I just did that."

"It was great," he said with a huge grin.

When Giuseppe returned, he brought our drinks, and took our order before hurrying back to the kitchen. I took a sip of my wine, savoring the richness of the vintage before I swallowed. "Can I ask you a question?"

"Sure." He set down his beer and leaned back in his chair.

"Did you and Charlie ever date?"

He gave that devastatingly handsome crooked grin that made my knees knock together and my heart skip like ten beats. "No. Like I said to her once upon a time, I thought we would've had fun together, but I never had major romantic feelings for her. In the spirit of full disclosure, however, we did kiss once."

My spine stiffened as I slid my fingers down the stem of my glass. "You did?"

"Yeah," he said still smiling like an idiot. "Almost a year ago after the championship match, she was making a fool of herself in front of Jensen, who was there with a date. I stepped up to save her from complete and utter humiliation."

I shook my head. "How chivalrous of you." After I swallowed a sip of my wine, I let the glass linger near my lips.

"I'm always here to help." His eyes dropped to my lips for a second before snapping back to my eyes. "My turn to ask a question."

I sat as tall as I could in my seat. "What do you want to know?"

"How many men have you dated since Harper's father?"

My body itched to squirm and shift around. "None, and please don't call him that."

He didn't skip a beat. "You're kidding, right?"

"About which part," I said in a bit of a higher tone.

"I suppose both."

"Sawyer and I were together for part of the pregnancy—until he realized I wasn't going to change my mind about keeping her. I was still pretty broken-hearted when she was born. I'd considered naming her Sawyer, but Gram threatened me with bodily harm if I did."

"I like your grandmother more and more every day." He took a sizeable swallow of his beer, set it down, and propped his forearms upon the table. "But Harper is six. You haven't dated at all?"

"Not even a fling. If you remember, I did mention that I was too caught up finishing a degree and working toward a decent income for the two of us. A love life was never a priority."

"I think your grandmother likes me."

With a laugh, I nodded. "She does. Harper seems to like you too. She told me I should marry you." Let's see how this jolted his long-time bachelor brain.

 Much to my dismay, his grin only grew. "I think she gives amazing advice." Were there any teeth in his head that I couldn't see right now? Sheesh! Talk about an overblown grin.

"One kiss and you're ready for marriage?"

He rotated his bottle of beer in its place. "I'd like to date some first, but sure, why not?"

"Because we hardly know each other. That's why." Ack! Why was my voice so high? So he didn't react the way I'd expected. Did I have to let on that I was shocked?

He reached over and snagged my hand, his thumb tracing maddening circles around my palm. "We've known each other for over a year now and talked from time to time. It's not like we're complete strangers."

"Yes, but you don't know the little things, like my favorite color or favorite food."

"Blue," he said without so much as blinking. "Your favorite color is blue. I don't think you have a favorite shade because I've seen you wear just about every hue."

I dropped against the back of my chair with a thud. "Okay, Mr. Know-it-all, what about my favorite food."

"See, that's more difficult. We've never eaten together before. I see you all the time at the grocery store, but you mostly have whole foods in your basket and very little that's processed—probably to make it easier to cook for Harper."

"I hate reading labels. If it's simply broccoli, I don't have to worry about whether it has nuts in it."

Without my hand to torment, he crossed his arms over his chest while he relaxed back into his seat. "Your friend Mei had some interesting information. She commented that you love General Tso's chicken, but you rarely order it."

I would need to pinch Mei for revealing my guilty splurge. "If I order shrimp lo mein, Harper and I share and nothing is fried. General Tso's is pretty fattening."

He steepled his hands in front of his chest like he was some evil villain. "Did I guess correctly?"

"It's *one* of my favorites."

"You're not going to make this easy on me, are you?" Despite his words, he wasn't upset. The slight curve of his lips hinted that he was enjoying the chase. His gaze locked onto mine and held, making this scorching heat spread from my chest up to my cheeks. It was disturbing how he could do that with so little effort.

A bowl appeared in my line of vision, breaking the spell. "The arugula salad," said Giuseppe, setting the dish down, followed by small plates so we could share. After inquiring whether we needed anything, he departed in the direction of the kitchen.

We dished out our salad, and I diverted our conversation to topics that wouldn't make me turn brilliant shades of red before his very eyes. I started by commenting on the ducks that always swam along the river, which brought the discussion to next week's weather followed by when Charlie would return to work, and so on. By the time we paid the bill and were walking out the door, I hadn't just eaten salad and pizza. Elliot had somehow weakened my defenses and talked me into the Tiramisù.

After being in the air conditioning for the last two hours, the warmth of the evening slapped me in the face as soon as we walked outside. We hadn't exactly been in a hurry and talked more than we ate at times. "I'm stuffed. I can't believe you ordered that Tiramisù."

His hand slipped against mine, our fingers entwining. "I saw your eyes light up when Giuseppe mentioned it. You might not have been willing to admit it, but you did want it. Besides, the best part was the look on your face and that little moan you made when you took the first bite. You sure make being a gentleman difficult when you do that." The last was said close to my ear, his breath skittering along my flesh and prickling the skin.

Giuseppe's was near the beginning of the Riverwalk, so we took our time and browsed through some of the small shops until we reached the end. Elliot pulled me past the paved sidewalk and down the sloped trail to the bend where the water gurgled over rocks as it turned to curve along the edge of the historic district of town. Further on, expensive neighborhoods ruined the wild look I loved about this part of the river, but this wooded section was a small off-shoot of a park, keeping it safe from development.

"Do you want to see where I live?"

"Sure," I said as I peered down the trail that followed the river.

We picked our way along the path until enough of the trees cleared for a good-sized house. Multi-paned windows trimmed in white covered the front which faced out toward the river, and a set of stone steps led down to the water's edge.

"It looks almost new." My voice was softer. As far as I knew, no one could build along this part of the river. All the buildings on the Riverwalk had been there for ages and restored to house the businesses and restaurants that flourished along the path.

That low rumble in his chuckle tugged at something low in my stomach. "It was a heap when I bought it a few years ago, and I had to get permission from the county. They wanted to make sure I wasn't cutting down any trees or ripping down what was there to build something new. The house is essentially what it was before only in better condition. I did add the windows along the front and the stone steps."

"How long did it take you?"

"I worked on it a little at a time. The inside was done during the winter, and I worked on the windows and the outside during spring and summer. Last year, I replaced the roof. Ellie's husband helped me with solar and wind power and the grants and incentives to help pay for it. There were no powerlines and it was impossible to get someone to install them because it would be costly to run electrical so far from the main lines."

He led the way inside to a cozy living room with warm wood floors and a plush grey sectional with white throw pillows. A huge oriental style rug adorned the floor and gave a slight pop of color. I loved the stained beams in the high ceiling.

"It was pretty much all open to begin with, so I left it like that."

No doors separated the kitchen, living room, and dining room. They didn't even have full walls separating them, but the colors coordinated from the consistent flooring to the grey cabinets and stained wood countertops, to the matching oriental style rug under the dining room table.

"It's great," I said, running a hand along the countertop.

"Thanks." He shoved his hands in his pockets and looked around. "Would you like a glass of wine? We could sit outside now that it's cooler."

"That sounds really nice."

He pulled a bottle of Merlot from one of the cabinets and uncorked it like a pro. Once he'd poured me a glass, he pulled a local craft beer from the fridge, took my hand, and led me outside. "Would you hold my beer a moment?"

He went back inside and came out a moment later with some large cushions that he put on a swing hanging from one of the huge trees. No doubt the cushions wouldn't last and would mildew if left outside in the South Carolina weather. Once he'd set it all up, we both settled in and sipped our drinks while the setting sun began to dim our surroundings.

"Did you check on Harper and your grandmother?"

"When I went to the bathroom at Giuseppe's."

His free arm slipped around my shoulders and his thumb skimmed my bare shoulder. Why could I feel that touch everywhere? Forget that—how could someone take control of my body with so little effort? I'd never experienced anything like it. Not that I had a vast knowledge of men, but this was new.

"Gram fussed at me and told me to go enjoy myself."

His chest shook as he scooted a little closer. "Was she the same when you were growing up?"

"Pretty much." I took a sip of wine and leaned against him. "Even when she's on her deathbed, she'll still be telling everyone what to do and insisting she can walk the length of a football field."

"I think it's amazing. Without her, you wouldn't be so independent and determined to succeed on your own terms."

"That's true, I suppose."

At some point while we'd been talking the crickets began singing from the trees around us. "Do you hear that?" I whispered.

"I love it," he said softly. "This is my favorite time of day to sit out here." After another moment of listening to the crickets' music, he took a sip of his beer and propped the bottle on his leg. "I start at that physical therapy clinic in town tomorrow."

"I can't believe you didn't tell me." I pulled my legs up onto the swing so I faced him. "Are you excited?"

"Well, yeah. It's what I've wanted for a while now. I'd done some of my clinicals there, and it's really laid back. It's a great atmosphere."

An impulse had my palm pressing on his thigh. "I'm happy for you."

"Thanks." We sat quietly and sipped our drinks while we listened to the local nightlife. Elliot's fingers trailed along the top of my hand where it still rested on his leg, increasing that crazy hum in my body with each grazing stroke. As soon as my glass was empty, he took it and set it on the ground with his bottle.

He sat up, drew me closer, and nuzzled his nose near my temple. "Maggie." My name came softly from his lips. When I turned, my eyes met his and refused to look away. Gentle fingers combed back the side of my hair. "You're so beautiful."

His lips descended slowly to mine in a delicate kiss, as though my lips were made of a paper-thin glass rather than flesh. I leaned further in and deepened what he'd started. Fingers that had brushed along my hair and grazed my arm didn't hesitate to entwine with mine as he deepened the kiss. His arm moved from behind me so his hand could cup the back of my head.

He drew back for a moment, and I opened my eyes to find him watching me. His maddening fingers caressed my arms, shredding my patience. I grabbed the lapel of his shirt and pulled him back, opening my mouth under his lips and flicking my tongue against his.

God, I'd missed this! How long had it been since I'd kissed a man or even let one hold my hand? Gram was right. In that time, I'd forgotten I was more than Harper's mother—that I could be more. To be honest, I hadn't wanted to remember what I was missing, or I would've wallowed in a tremendous tub of Ben and Jerry's for the last six years.

His lips made their way along my jaw to my neck where they planted several suckling kisses that made me moan and shift my legs over his.

I wanted his lips on mine again, so I steered his face so I could claim them. His hand landed upon my thigh and squeezed. His lips were soft, and while it sounded crazy, I wanted him to never stop kissing me.

We did nothing more than kiss while the night enveloping us grew darker. At times, his fingers would wander to my hair, wrapping a curl around his finger or combing it back. Then, he'd return his hand to my leg, but it never strayed further.

When he finally drew back, he smiled with this peaceful expression that tugged at my heart. He glanced toward the water. "Look," he said, pointing.

I gasped when I set eyes on what had to be a hundred tiny blinking lightning bugs flashing in the trees across the river. "I don't think I've ever seen so many at one time."

"They inhabit the woods from the bend at the end of the Riverwalk to that new subdivision on the other side of the park. I took a kayak out one night and rowed along the river with them to light the way. It was phenomenal." His tone was breathless.

I laid my head on his shoulder while we watched the little blinking lights flickering in and out of the trees. I couldn't remember the last time I hadn't worried about a single thing: Harper, Gram, paying an unexpected bill, or dealing with some crazy demand for a wedding. But tonight, my brain cleared, my heart settled, and I found peace.

Chapter 7

I pressed my lips together to keep from screaming while I waited until the footsteps leaving my office faded and the outer door closed. Only then did I let my head drop onto my desk. She had to be kidding, right? The bride who'd just left had seemed such a normal human being when we'd first met. Who would've thought she'd turn into the bride of Satan?

My cell phone rang, and I lifted my head enough to barely make out Elliot's picture on the screen. I grabbed the phone and answered while I set my forehead back on the desk. "Hi."

"Uh, oh. You okay?"

"No, I had a meeting with a demanding bride. I won't be able to go to lunch today. I'm sorry. Between helping Ellie cover Jena and Charlie's clients and this woman completely overhauling her reception, there's no way I'll get out of here before five."

"What about Harper?"

"Shit! You'd think that I'd be used to not having Gram pick her up yet." Gram might be refusing to use the walker around the house, but she knew better than to try to make that walk without help.

"Can I pick her up for you?"

"You're not on the approved list. I don't have to call and arrange for Gram, Mei, or me. Besides, what about your job? You just started at the clinic on Monday."

"I'm around the corner from the elementary school. What if Mei picks up Harper and drops her by the office on her way home. That way, I don't miss work."

He had a point. Mei would walk out of her way to get to me. Elliot's clinic was on her route. "Okay, that will work. I'll call her."

"I'll let the ladies at the front desk know."

"Thank you," I said softly.

"Hey, Harper is a lot of fun, and I'm glad I can help."

I smiled despite the load of work waiting for me when I hung up. "I've gotta go. I need to bang my head on the desk another five or six times before I call the caterers."

"Don't do too much damage. I think your face is pretty gorgeous the way it is. If you'd like, I can kiss the bruises away later." His voice had dropped all low and intimate, making my tummy flip.

"I hope you're alone."

"I'm in my office, but I do have a client in two minutes."

"Bye," I said softly.

"Bye, Mags."

As soon as the line clicked, I lifted my head and found the photo that popped up when he'd called. I hadn't even known he'd programmed himself into my phone until the first time he'd called me. My sneaky daughter must've keyed in my passcode for him so he could take a selfie and make himself a contact.

He'd taken it on the back porch at some point while we were working on the deck since he wore his gym shorts and a t-shirt. The best part was the sexy lop-sided grin he wore while he lifted the edge of his shirt, revealing a small part of his six-pack abs.

"Maggie?"

I jumped about a mile and flipped my phone face down on the desk. "Yeah?" My hand slipped along my chin. I'd have been horrified if Ellie had noticed I was drooling.

"I overheard Miss Steele as she was leaving. Which caterer were you using?"

"Garnish. James has already bent over backwards accommodating her original requests. He's going to be pissed."

"He won't take it out on you. She's not the first temperamental client he's dealt with." Ellie leaned against the door frame, her long, flowy skirt draping to one side. "Don't worry. She's close to the point of no return." That was our euphemism for the final date stipulated in the client's contract for any changes.

"Don't say that. I'm willing to bet a large sum of money that she'll call me the day before to change the reception venue or the menu for the fourth time."

She giggled and pushed herself from her resting spot. "Call James. See what he can do. If you have any issues, I'm happy to help."

"Thanks!"

❧⟵⋯ ⋯⟶☙

In the end, James and I commiserated over Miss Steele, who seemed like the sweetest thing on Earth upon first acquaintance, but would devour your first born if you weren't careful.

My stomach growled, and I picked up my coffee cup only to find there wasn't one miniscule drop remaining. "Crap," I muttered. I'd held high hopes that amazing liquid gold would tide me over until I could arrange food.

"Hey, beautiful."

78

I'd just made to stand when Elliot's voice almost caused me trip over the corner of my desk. "What are you doing here?"

"Well, I have a lunch hour, so I thought I'd bring you something." He held a handled paper shopping bag in front of his chest. "Hungry?"

"Starving! You're a life saver."

He walked inside, sat the bag on my desk, and dropped into one of the chairs. "Things looking better?"

"A little." I picked up the bag and took a peek, revealing a takeaway carton from Starlight nestled inside.

"Elliot?"

We both pivoted quickly to Ellie in the doorway. "Hi," said Elliot with a small wave. "How are you?"

"I'm great, thanks. I didn't know the two of you were acquainted." She had this odd glint in her eye as she glanced back and forth between us—and back and forth again.

I scratched my fingers up through the hair at my neck a couple of times "We are."

"We worked out together this morning. Maggie told me she probably wouldn't get to eat lunch, so I brought her something. She exercised too hard to skip a meal."

"Ah." One side of Ellie's lips curved. "Very thoughtful of you." I'd be willing to bet just about anything that Ellie suspected ulterior motives. "I'm heading next door to feed the baby. If you need me, I have my phone."

"Thanks."

As soon as she left, Elliot chuckled and stood, walking around my desk and turning my chair so I faced him. He leaned forward with his hands on the arm rests. "You're cute when you're embarrassed."

79

"I've never been comfortable with my personal life coming into work. Harper has only been here once or twice during office hours. I've always tried to keep this separate from my personal life."

"Relax," he said softly. "I'm not offended, but I'm sure Charlie and the other girls wonder why you feel the need to be so strict with yourself. They've geared this company so they can do as they wish in regards to family. They wouldn't hold Harper or even me against you."

"Charlie has said as much. I really didn't know them that well when I started here. That's definitely changed, but I'm not an owner like they are. I never wanted to assume I could do as they do."

"That makes sense." He planted a quick kiss on my lips, drawing away and backing toward the door with a toothy grin. "Harper and I will be here at closing for you. We're planning dinner, so be ready and don't plan on working late."

"What?" Before I could ask the multitude of questions that sprang to the tip of my tongue, he was gone. I still don't know how he made it out the front exit so quickly. When I ran out to the steps, he waved back at me. What was he up to? I supposed I would discover that at five o'clock. One thing was certain, I definitely wasn't used to this upheaval in my structured day to day life.

When I returned inside, I grabbed utensils from the kitchen and a bottle of sparkling mineral water. After I sat down, I quickly called Mei, who was happy to pick up Harper and take her to the physical therapy clinic. Then, I organized my clients on my computer while I ate, updating certain accounts and making a note of the most pressing business for the afternoon.

The rest of the day flew by, but I never had a free moment to really think about the time or how long until closing. I startled when the bell rang on the front door, followed by a "Mommy! We're here!" Harper's feet pounded along the hardwood floors and rattled the entire downstairs and probably some of Jena's home upstairs.

When she sailed around the corner of my office, her backpack slapped against her shoulders. I'd barely managed to turn before she barreled into my arms with Elliot following not far behind. "Are you ready to go?"

"Hi, Harper," said Ellie, standing in the door with her son Jacob. "You've grown like a weed since I saw you last." That was true. I'd always relied on help from Gram and Mei, I finished work at home, or Ellie simply wasn't here on those few occasions Harper came to the office after school.

"I'm in first grade now." Harper held up the one finger for emphasis while Jacob gave a big toothless grin. "I like your baby." She skipped over and bounced his little sock clad feet, making him giggle. "Mommy, I want a little sister. I suppose a brother would be okay, but if I have a sister, we can share toys."

Elliot looked at the floor while his shoulders shook. Meanwhile, I'm sure I coughed several times in a useless attempt to respond to her sudden demand. "I don't know, Harp. I—"

Ellie stood watching the fallout with nearly the same expression she wore earlier. I wasn't trying to hide anything, but when she turned and arched that one not-so-subtle eyebrow at me, my face caught on fire.

"What are we doing for dinner?" Maybe that would change the direction of the conversation!

"It's a surprise," said Harper before she turned to Elliot. "Can we go? I can't wait to show her."

I grabbed my Burberry plaid purse and started to follow them as they made their way toward the front door.

"Have fun, guys!" called Ellie before snagging my hand and saying in a soft voice, "Way to go, Maggie. He's a catch, you know. You'll have the ladies of Marysville wishing you bodily harm when they find out."

I pressed my palms to my cheeks. "Ellie—"

"No, you deserve to be happy. Don't close yourself off. You've done that for long enough." She pushed me by the shoulder. "Now go get your groove back before he returns to see why you aren't close behind."

When I stepped outside, Elliot waited on the porch while Harper hopped down the last step then turned to hop back up. He reached for my hand and drew me closer. "Anything wrong?"

"No, Ellie wanted a quick word." Harper grabbed Elliot's other hand, and if I could've done Ellie's single eyebrow lift, I would've certainly used it at that moment.

"Do you mind leaving your car? Harper said she prefers to walk."

"No, I can leave it."

As we walked through the park, I listened to Elliot and Harper debate nonsense like whether the swings were better than the slides, or why Harper preferred the merry-go-round at the school.

Why did it bother me that everyone, including Ellie, claimed that I'd closed myself off? I had, but I hadn't recognized it until Gram accused me of it. Now, everyone seemed to say it as well.

We turned right at the other side of the park, and I hesitated. "The house is in the other direction."

"We aren't going home," said Harper with an impish grin.

Elliot smiled and tipped his head toward the Riverwalk. "Come on. It'll be fun. I promise."

The moment we started down the steps down to the riverside path, I stopped. "Elliot, I'm not sure about this." I always carried an epi-pen, but that didn't mean I wanted to tempt fate.

He put his arm around my shoulder and pulled me close right as Mrs. Jennings from the ice cream parlor passed. Had that soft trill been a giggle? I had to shake that off. I simply couldn't think about whether the biggest gossip in town would tell the entire county by sunrise. I had to consider Harper.

"I spoke with Giuseppe when we were there Sunday," he said softly before I could freak out further. "Pesto is only served on the specials menu, so they don't serve it every day. He also assured me there are no nuts in any of the other recipes, and that if we called ahead, he'd even bake her some bread in a separate oven to be on the safe side."

"Seriously?" It all sounded too good to be true.

"I promise. I asked Harper this afternoon if she wanted to try, and she was so excited. I don't mean to step on your toes. You have to know I wouldn't bring the two of you here if I thought she'd be hurt in any way. She even said she has an epi-pen in her backpack."

I bit my lip. "Just so you know, the office at school isn't aware of that one. It's in the event she has a reaction at Mei's or on a field trip. The school has one, but you're supposed to have a second dose in case it's needed."

"I do know that from my training, so I believe it's safe to assume you have an epi-pen in your purse. You also have a former EMT if you need it. I think we're set."

A laugh bubbled up from my throat. "You've covered every possible issue."

That wicked grin appeared. "I've tried."

As soon as we stepped inside, Giuseppe called a greeting to us from the back of the dining room, his arms open wide as though he intended to bestow an enormous hug; however, instead of hugging, he simply spoke loudly in his thick accent as he ushered us to a table in the back corner. "Don't you worry, Mama. I have a big kitchen here with an entire part we only use to cook tomato sauce. I take food for allergies back there and make it for special customers. I can show you, if you like."

Even with his thick accent, his willingness to prove himself kept me from losing my mind. "Thank you for the offer, but I don't want to put out your kitchen staff."

"Can I see?" Harper glanced between us.

"Of course," boomed Giuseppe, "why don't we ask what Mama and Papa want to drink. You can help me bring it out to them."

"He's not my Papa yet." Harper peeked back at us. "He's just Elliot right now."

Elliot pulled me to sit beside him in the booth and laughed in the most infuriating way while he ordered a craft beer for himself and the same wine I'd had on Sunday for me. He kissed my cheek and put his arm around my shoulders. "Mags, you haven't stopped blushing all day."

I turned to slightly face him. "I can't believe you find this so funny."

He leaned in toward my ear. "That Ellie can tell something is going on?"

"Well, yeah."

"And that Harper has grand plans for me to be her father?"

"Of course," I responded. "Most men would run screaming."

"Firstly, I don't care who knows I like you, but I suspect this is uncomfortable because it's something you haven't had to deal with in a long time." He pressed a quick kiss to my lips. "Lastly, I take it as a compliment that Harper wants me to be her dad. The reason I laugh is how quickly you turned beet red. With your complexion, that shade is no small feat. There's also the fact that she announced in the middle of your office that she wants a little sister. The best part was that I could tell she's never said that to you before."

I opened my mouth to speak, but he covered it with his. As soon as I relaxed and began kissing him back—chastely since we were in public—he withdrew. "You have an incredible daughter. I admired you before I knew her. Since I've gotten to know her, I admire you even more."

Damned if my cheeks didn't get hot again!

After an eventless dinner, Harper walked between Elliot and me, holding each of our hands. Gram was in her room when we arrived home, so I checked in on her. She'd had a friend keep her company for the majority of the day and was now spending some quiet time knitting.

"Harp, run upstairs and take a bath," I said when I walked back into the living room. "We'll need to get your homework done before you go to bed."

She put her lunch box on the counter. "Elliot helped me earlier."

"Okay, then take your bath and put your pajamas on. It's nearly bedtime anyway." She ran up the stairs while I opened the fridge to consider what she was going to have for lunch tomorrow.

Two hands snuck around my waist, and Elliot hugged me from behind, his lips caressing that spot under my ear that made me shiver as though the room was cold.

"Thank you for tonight. Harper had an amazing time."

"I hope you did too." His voice was low before his attention returned to my neck. Goosebumps prickled down my spine, making me squirm.

I shut the fridge and sighed. I'd worry about Harper's lunch in the morning. I turned in Elliot's arms, pressing my lips to his. Before I knew what was happening, he'd lifted me to the countertop and stepped between my legs, drawing me flush to him.

Little feet pounded upstairs, and he paused, glancing up as a door slammed. "We only have a few more minutes." My darned voice was weird and raspy again.

His fingers slipped under the edge of my blouse and stroked the flesh above the waistband of my skirt, which was now hiked indecently up my thighs. At the first footstep on the stairs, he lifted me down and stepped back before Harper burst into the kitchen. "I'm ready for bed!" She skipped forward and jumped into my arms for a hug. I was lucky I caught her since I was still in a daze.

"Love you, Sweet Pea."

She kissed my cheek. "Love you." As soon as her feet hit the floor, she took off for Elliot and jumped at him just as she did me. "Thank you for taking me to Giuseppe's."

"You're quite welcome," he said.

She kissed him on the cheek. "Will you pick me up from school sometimes?"

"If you want me to, I don't mind. I'll talk to Mommy about it. Okay?"

After a nod, she hopped down and ran back upstairs. "Good night," she called down while her feet pounded on the steps.

"I guess I should go." When I turned back to Elliot, he scratched the back of his neck awkwardly.

"Not quite yet," I said. Without further explanation, I grabbed his hand and tugged him up the stairs behind me.

Chapter 8

As soon as I closed my bedroom door, I pressed Elliot against it and slipped my arms around his neck. "Maggie?" he said right before my lips claimed his. I had no idea who deepened the kiss, but I groaned and slipped my hands under his shirt, yanking it over his head. My hands slid up his chest and down his arms. He took my hand and interlaced our fingers. At that moment, something inside me jolted awake—something that had been dormant for so long. I broke the kiss.

"I . . ." As I started to shift back, Elliot grabbed me and held me where I was.

"No, you're not withdrawing. Tell me what's wrong."

I took a huge breath and did my best to look directly at him. "I don't know."

"Are you sure?"

I took a long, slow breath, filling my lungs, while I closed my eyes. "Since we began seeing one another, Gram, Charlie, and Ellie have all commented about how I've closed myself off." I couldn't believe I'd told him that. "I suddenly feel different. I can't explain it."

His fingers trailed up and down my spine, though they never strayed lower than my waistline. Those small caresses helped relax me. "You were hurt by Harper's father—"

"Don't call him that." I shook my head and resituated myself a bit. "He gave away any right he had to be called that."

"Agreed. Is sperm donor better?"

I couldn't help when one side of my lips twitched upward. "Infinitely."

"Okay, so you were hurt by that weasel of a sperm donor and needed to get your life together for yourself and Harper. That's not a small task. I think what you've managed to accomplish is amazing. I admire the hell out of you for it."

"Thanks."

My gaze remained locked onto his chest, but he wouldn't let me avoid him and lifted my chin. "Is that why you've been more open to me lately?"

"Yes, and to be honest, I've always been attracted to you."

"Oh, yeah?" His eyebrows waggled, and his voice was a tinge higher. "How attracted?"

I pinched his side. "Ow," he said, laughing. He slid down the wall, pulling me with him until I was straddling his lap.

"Today was just like a normal day. We worked out like we've been doing lately, but after, when everything fell apart, you brought me lunch, you helped me by watching Harper—"

"Honestly, Harper isn't a chore. She's an easy kid. She took out her own homework, and the ladies at the front desk loved her. She sat with them while she worked. When she was done with her homework, they printed out coloring sheets and hung the finished products all over their workspace. I only checked on her between appointments."

My heart filled my chest so it was difficult to breathe. I tried not to think of Sawyer most of the time, yet the fact that Elliot didn't think Harper was difficult while Sawyer had refused any and all responsibility made me want Elliot all the more. I leaned forward and kissed him hard before I pulled back.

"Regardless, she had a great time with you. She also adored Giuseppe's. I've become so fearful of taking her places, so I don't ask if restaurants can accommodate her. You gave her something new." My darned eyes burned and made me blink rapidly. "This evening, I was simply happier than I can remember being in forever."

"And it made you want to bring me to your room and kiss me?" He gave a smug nod. "Good to know. Any time I want to kiss you, I simply need to blow your mind. Seems a decent compromise."

I covered my face and shook my head. "You can be so ridiculous sometimes."

He pulled my hands away and squeezed them gently. "Life is serious enough. Besides, I love to hear you laugh." He twirled one of my curls around his finger. "I love your hair. It's so soft." He gently caressed across my collar bone. "Your skin is too." He paused where my top had shifted to the side. "When did you get sun?"

I glanced down to where the skin was slightly fairer under my top. "I suppose when we worked on the deck."

I peered around at the wood floor. "You can't be comfortable like this."

"I have you in my lap," he said seriously, "and I'm touching you. I could sit here until my butt goes numb." His eyes held mine while his fingertips skimmed along my waistband.

I took his hands and stood, pulling so he would join me. As soon as his feet hit the floor, he refused to release my hands. "Why did you bring me up here?"

"I wanted to kiss you where Gram and Harper couldn't interrupt."

He pressed his lips to mine softly. "Then I should go."

He made to turn, but I pulled him back. "Stay with me?"

"Are you sure?"

I had to shake off the effects of his hands softly caressing up and down my arms. There was no way I could speak without embarrassing myself, so I nodded. I cleared my throat. "I should get ready." I pointed awkwardly at the bathroom.

After one last peck, he released me so I could brush my teeth, which I accomplished in record time. When I returned to the room, he was holding a picture frame from my bedside table.

"My parents," I said.

He smiled and nodded. "I figured. I can't tell who you resemble more."

"Most people say I look like my dad."

"Except you have a lighter skin tone and your mother's eyes."

I took the photo from his hand and gave it a fond look. "That's what Gram always says."

As I returned the frame to its spot, Elliot took off his pants, revealing boxer briefs that clung to an ass worthy of showing off. My eyes trailed down to his toned legs. He wasn't one of those men who worked only his upper body and had twigs for legs. He turned around and scratched the back of his head. "You didn't change."

"Not yet." I stepped closer, my fingers reaching out to touch the muscles along the side of his ribs. He was so beautiful. "Wait a minute," he said with a low chuckle. "What about you? You've seen nearly all of me. Do I get to see more of you?"

My teeth sank into my lip as I reached for the buttons on my blouse.

"May I?" At my nod, he started at the bottom, slowly releasing each button, and shifted the material apart when he reached the top. "God, I love black lace," he breathed at the sight of my bra.

His fingertips trailed around my shoulders and stomach until I took his hand and pressed his palm over my breast. After squeezing and rubbing over the tip, he shivered and kissed me. "What do you want, Maggie?"

"I want you to hold me. Do you think you could leave before Harper wakes up?"

He brushed my curls over my shoulder. "Sure, if that's what you want. What about your grandmother?"

"Gram won't care, but I don't want Harper to ask questions yet."

He reached for the fastenings on my skirt, and I froze. He stopped and cradled my cheek. "You're nervous about me seeing more of you, aren't you?"

"Yeah," I said. "It's been a long time."

He ran the tip of his finger down my stomach. "You make it sound like you're ancient. I promise there isn't one part of you that I won't like."

"You can't promise that." I couldn't help but giggle tightly.

"Oh, I can. Let me show you." He loosened my white and black floral skirt and slipped it over my hips. I'd never quite gotten my lower stomach as flat as it was before Harper, and I had a small set of stretchmarks on either side of my bellybutton. I know you're supposed to own those "tiger stripes," but I'd never quite managed that much confidence. "You're stunning. Do you know how sexy you are?"

His lips pressed against mine and coaxed them as well as the rest of me to forget why I'd been nervous in the first place. "Would you be more comfortable wearing nightclothes?"

I shook my head. The intensity of his gaze when he studied my body made me inhale and unhook my bra, letting it slide down my arms to the floor.

Elliot touched his forehead to mine while he looked at my breasts. "We better get you under the covers before I rip those panties off and make you mine."

"Do you want to brush your teeth?" I pressed him back a step. "I have an extra toothbrush in the top drawer.

"Yes, that'd be great."

While he brushed his teeth, I removed the throw pillows from the bed and drew down the comforter. I didn't think to ask if he had a favorite side. I usually slept in the center unless Harper climbed into the bed during the night, which hadn't happened in a few months. In any event, when he returned, we both climbed in a side and met in the middle, our legs entwining and holding hands.

"Do you have plans for the weekend?" he asked quietly once I'd dimmed the lamp.

"No, I hadn't given it much thought. Why?"

"Why don't you and Harper stay at my house? We can kayak on Saturday, grill, and roast marshmallows over the firepit."

"That sounds amazing, but what about Gram? It's one thing to leave her alone for a work day, but an entire weekend is a long time. I'm also sure she'd like to go to church on Sunday."

He shrugged. "We could bring her out for the day, so she's not so alone. I'm not sure I have a place where she could sleep comfortably. All the bedrooms are upstairs."

I shifted a teensy bit closer. "Before she broke her hip, she could climb stairs. She preferred to have her bedroom downstairs because it was easier. We simply put in a door from the small study downstairs to the three-quarter bath off the laundry room. It made more sense. A bench in the shower was less problematic than the tub upstairs."

"The move was probably necessary. If y'all hadn't moved her, she probably would've broken her hip earlier." He yawned before he kissed my thumb. "Maybe part of Saturday, then?" His voice trailed off some while he spoke. Soon, his eyelashes twitched as his breathing evened.

Something inside broke and flooded my chest with warmth as I watched him. To tell the truth, I'd hardly resisted him since that day we went to lunch together. Was that only a few short weeks ago? At some point, my heart had beat my mind into submission and let him inside.

Carefully, so I didn't wake him, I reached behind me and turned off the lamp. I rolled onto my side and backed against him. Only a moment later, his arms and body wrapped around me from behind with a "mmm."

The next morning, I was prepping Harper's lunch when Gram hobbled in with two canes. I wasn't sure how Elliot had convinced her to use those when she'd begun to adamantly refuse the walker; however, I sure wasn't going to question it.

She still wasn't as strong as she'd been before surgery. I was thankful she'd finally listened to someone.

"I caught Elliot skulking out of the house this morning."

A grimace, no doubt, crossed my face. Like I'd told Elliot, Gram wouldn't care. I didn't mention that I'd hear about it for weeks on end. "I doubt he was 'skulking' as you put it, and nothing happened."

"That's a shame."

I stopped stacking ham on the bread and gaped. "Gram!"

"You're a grown woman, Margaret—one with a child. It wouldn't be the first time, and that man is as attractive as they come. If I were your age, I'd throw him down and go for it. The two of you have been seeing each other for a couple of weeks now, since my surgery, and you were a bit more than casual acquaintances for longer. You wouldn't exactly be rushing into anything."

"It's taken me some time to figure things out."

"You mean you've been fighting with yourself."

"Not as much as I would've thought. I'm not second-guessing anymore."

She gave a curt nod and sat on one of the barstools. "Good. The two of you ought to get away for a weekend some time."

"I can't simply leave you and Harper. Not yet."

"Oh, please. Amy Louise can stay for a night or two. She's been pretty lonely since her husband died. You know her son lives in California and rarely visits. She comes by most days while you're at work anyway."

Amy Louise Harlan was fifteen years younger than Gram and still got around really well. Three months ago, her husband had a massive heart attack without any warning. The entire town knew "poor Amy Louise" and her situation.

"Could Amy Louise spend this weekend with you?"

"So soon?" Gram asked her little body shooting taller in her seat.

"Not quite. Elliot asked if Harper and I wanted to spend the weekend at his house. We'd go kayaking on the river and roast marshmallows over the firepit." I hadn't considered that I'd actually be able to go. With Gram's offer, it was as if the sun had emerged from the clouds.

Harper came running down the stairs, her Stitch backpack on her back until she dumped it by the door. "Gram, can you braid my hair?"

"Of course, I can." Gram pivoted her stool while Harper climbed onto the one next to her. "What will it be today?"

"Two braids up the back to buns, please." After she placed a case of hair paraphernalia on the counter, she put her hands up high on the sides of her head, mimicking buns.

Gram's eyes shifted to me as Harper bent over so Gram could part her hair down the middle. "Did you have a good day yesterday?"

I kept preparing Harper's lunch while I listened.

"It was the best! Ms. Mei picked me and Lu from school and took me to Elliot's office. I sat in front with the receptists and did my homework and colored."

"You did?" Gram's voice held that note of wonder that always kept my daughter rambling like there was no tomorrow. "What was Elliot doing?"

"He saw patience—"

"Patients?" I asked emphasizing the "t" at the end.

"Patients," she repeated. "Then he asked me about going to Giuseppe's."

Gram finished the first French braid and started the second. "That Italian place on the river?"

"Yeah, that one. I got to go into the kitchen and see where he made my food, and I helped Mr. Giuseppe get our drinks." My grandmother looked over with raised eyebrows.

"Elliot explained Harper's nut allergy last weekend and called ahead yesterday to make sure pesto wasn't on the specials menu. Giuseppe made Harper's food in a prep kitchen they don't use much."

"How cool," Gram said, gushing. "Was the food good?" By the tone of her voice, she was asking Harper and not me this time.

"I had spaghetti and meatballs. It was awesome."

I smiled while I packed her lunch away in her lunch box.

Once that second braid was finished, it only took a moment for Gram to wind the rest into buns and pin them in place. "Do you want bows?" My daughter always refused to wear bows, but Gram loved teasing by asking if she wanted them.

"Gram, no!" Today, my daughter wore a pair of jeans and a white t-shirt with a blue and white checked flannel tied around her waist. No, my daughter ceased to be a girly dresser at about three or four; however, she still loved painted fingernails and her hair fixed.

"Here, go put this up," said Gram, handing Harper the case with hair bands and pins.

As soon as Harper was about half-way up the stairs, Gram snagged my hand when I set the lunch box to the side of the counter. "I'll call Amy Louise this morning. If she won't stay over, then I'll call the minister's wife. She stopped by and offered to help if I needed it."

"Just what I want." I crossed my arms over my chest. At Gram's frown, I huffed. "For the minister's wife to know I'm spending the night with a man. She's going to assume I'm having sex with him." I whispered the last.

"God, I hope you do." Gram followed, rolling her eyes. "Maybe you'll stop being so uptight about it."

"Harper! Are you ready? We need to go!"

"Are you meeting Elliot at the gym again?"

"No, he had an appointment at opening this morning."

Harper appeared at the foot of the stairs, which probably kept Gram from making whatever comment was coming next. Harper grabbed her backpack, I handed her the lunchbox, and after we both hugged Gram, we hurried out the door.

Chapter 9

"Harpsichord, would you please bring this to the kitchen?"

Elliot held out the empty salad bowl while Harper looked at him with wide eyes. "What's a harpschord?"

"It's like an old-fashioned piano that people played two hundred or so years ago."

She took the bowl from Elliot and grinned. "Okay."

As soon as she skipped inside, I smiled while I picked up the dirty knives and forks. "Charlie calls her Hardy har har, but no one else has nicknamed her that way."

"She seems to like it."

"She does. You joke around with her and those names make you sillier." We'd grilled marinated steaks, corn on the cob, and potato wedges that we ate outside. Now, the sun slowly descended as we cleaned up the table.

After Elliot picked up the last of the dishes, I followed him inside. "Harp?" Her head popped around the cabinets, her little eyes ringed with dark circles. Much to my surprise, she'd agreed to try fishing, so Elliot had worn her out fishing from the deck at the crack of dawn. We went kayaking after lunch. "Go take a bath and put on your pajamas."

"But Mommy, Elliot said we'd kayak after dark."

"I think we should pass on that tonight. Maybe we can do it another night."

"Anytime," said Elliot as he glanced up from loading the dishwasher. "You and your mommy are always welcome to stay with me. We can kayak whenever your mother says it's okay."

"I wanted to go tonight." I knew that whine well. I needed to get her in the bathtub before she melted down.

"Harper, if you continue to argue, you'll go straight to bed after your bath. If you take your bath without arguing, you can come outside and roast marshmallows first. Which do you want to choose?"

Her little shoulders slumped. "I'll take my bath."

"Do you remember how to turn on the water?" asked Elliot. After work on Friday, Harper and I went home, picked up our belongings, and drove over. Getting here by car was definitely different than walking from the Riverwalk.

"I do."

He dried his hands on a towel. "Why don't I make sure?"

"I know how!"

"Harper." My tone was low and firm.

"Sorry," she said, following him upstairs.

She'd been so excited when she'd seen the bedroom he had for her upstairs. Instead of using one of the actual bedrooms, he'd rigged up this fantastic tent in the loft with layers of fabric and fairy lights around a full-sized air mattress thrown on the floor. When he'd asked to borrow some of Gram's old quilts and flowery sheets, I'd wondered what he was up to. Now that I could see the finished product, I could only shake my head. It was incredible, and she absolutely adored it.

A moment later he returned. "She's tired."

"I know. We might want to get the dishwasher going so we can start the firepit. I don't think she'll last long past the first marshmallow."

By the time we'd finished the dishes and Elliot had lit the fire, Harper came outside in her pajamas and carrying a Stitch.

"Harmonica, come sit over here," said Elliot shifting a cut piece of tree trunk closer to the fire.

As she sat, she giggled softly. "You're silly."

Elliot handed her a skewer that was longer than any I'd ever seen. "You have a cool name, and I think it's fun to come up with unique nicknames. If you don't like it, you can always tell me and I'll stop."

"Did your daddy have nicknames for you?"

With a smile, Elliot put a marshmallow on her stick and helped her hold it near the fire. "He did. I played football, volleyball, and soccer so they were all sports related like 'pigskin' or 'jock-rabbit' because I could run quickly. I think anything that sounded goofy, he used."

"I can hold it myself." She looked up at Elliot, her tired eyes barely open. The sun was just going down, and I hoped she'd last long enough for the fireflies.

"Make sure you keep it near the flame, but not in it. You don't want to burn the marshmallow."

She nodded before she peered back up at him. "Elliot?"

"Yeah, Harper."

"I think the nicknames are funny. Mommy calls me Harp sometimes, so I don't mind."

He squatted back down next to her seat. "Cool. Just let me know if you change your mind. Okay?"

Sitting without interfering had been difficult. I'd told Elliot she loved the nicknames, but asking her input blew me away. Not to mention my six-year-old daughter was sitting next to an open flame, and I was twitching, waiting for her to fall or get burned. I trusted Elliot. I simply wasn't accustomed to someone behaving like Harper's father, which he'd done since we arrived at his house yesterday.

Harper had wanted him to read her a bedtime story last night. He made her breakfast before I woke up this morning, and he'd bought Harper a child-sized life jacket that he'd fitted for when we kayaked. He also put her in the double kayak with him, which made sense. He had a lot more practice than I had. She was safer with him.

These little bonding moments made my eyes burn and made me worry all at the same time. What if it didn't work out between us? Was I setting Harper up to be hurt as well?

My attention snapped back to them as Elliot grabbed something from the table. He opened a wrapper and broke two squares of what I then recognized as chocolate.

"Here, put your marshmallow between these."

She licked her little fingers when the gooey marshmallow squished between the chocolate. "Yum," she said, closing her eyes with a drawn-out sigh. Yeah, she was definitely my daughter.

Elliot guided her to stand and shifted back the stump. "Let's scoot you away from the fire so you don't get too hot." Once she was settled with her sticky treat, he sat with me on the swing and wrapped his arm around my shoulders.

"You're very quiet." His nose tickled my ear as he whispered.

"I was watching and thinking."

"Don't overthink things, Mags." He guided my chin around and kissed me gently on the lips but didn't linger. Instead, he turned back to make sure Harper was safe.

My head rested on his shoulder. "You do know my brain never stops."

"Then we'll have to find something more productive for it to think of."

That deep hum in his voice brought parts of my body to life. If he was attempting to distract me with sex, it would probably work. Last night, we'd had a glass of wine with dinner and one while we played Scrabble after Harper fell asleep. Once we'd climbed into his plush king-sized bed, we'd kissed and made out like teenagers for a while before Elliot tucked me against him and we'd fallen asleep. My body had been so revved up since he spent the night at my house that I was going to throw him down and do naughty things to him if he didn't do them to me first.

Harper was licking her fingers again, so I went over and picked up her stuffed toy before she ruined it. "Go wash your hands and brush your teeth."

She ran inside and the clomp, clomp, clomp of her feet pounding up the stairs echoed through the door. I sank back down on the swing with a sigh. "I keep waiting for her to put a hole through our stairs at home."

"I did the same thing when I was young," he said, kissing my forehead when I leaned back against him. "Didn't you?"

"Yeah, I guess I did."

His lips touched mine again in a gentle caress before he coaxed my lips open and took possession. My palm cradled his cheek as our lips meshed and our tongues tangled. His fingers dug into the sides of my faded denim cutoffs. Even though the temperature was cooler now than it was earlier in the day, I was far from cold. His body not only gave off heat, but our touching kept me warm from the inside as well.

Harper's stomps down the stairs broke us apart, though his arm remained around my shoulders. My daughter trotted over on her tiptoes—she was always on her tiptoes—and pulled herself up on the other side of Elliot. "Can I sit in your lap?"

"Of course." He removed his arm from me until she was situated on one leg with his opposite arm around her to ensure she didn't fall from the swing. That was when he pointed toward the forest on the opposite side of the river. "Look, across the water."

Her high-pitched gasp let us know when she saw them. "Lightning bugs," she said on an awed exhale. "Tons of them."

He wrapped his arm back around my shoulders and used his foot to rock us back and forth. I had no idea when Harper passed out, but five minutes later, her head rested against Elliot's chest, light snores coming from her open mouth.

"I'm going to put her in bed," he whispered. "I'll be right back. Don't move."

He was barely gone before he strode back outside like he was on a mission. "Those cutoffs have been making me crazy since you put them on this morning." When he reached the swing, he didn't sit. Instead, he leaned in and claimed my lips while pushing me back onto the cushion. His body covered mine, and my knees lifted to cradle him closer. Thank goodness the seat was wide enough, or we would've fallen.

We kissed, this time without restraint, which was easier when you didn't expect a six-year-old to come barreling out of the house. My fingers inched up the bottom of his shirt and slipped along his back, enjoying the solid feel of him against my palms. He unbuttoned and unzipped my shorts before his hands slid around the back under the waistline and my panties to grasp my rear.

I gasped as he pressed himself against me. When had that popped up? I abandoned his back and released the fastening on his cargo shorts so I could mimic what he was doing to me. I clenched his rear and pressed him down so he could grind that amazing hardness against me. It didn't take long before he pushed my cutoffs down some.

"Elliot?"

His fingers slipped around the front. "God, I need to feel you, Maggie. I need to know that you're wet for me." At the first touch, this incoherent noise burst from me and I lifted my hips in a silent plea for more. It'd been so long since I'd let a man touch me. Battery driven plastic didn't hold a candle to even the faintest touch from Elliot. Sawyer hadn't made my entire body buzz like it was at that moment.

"Don't stop."

His lips slammed against mine, and he groaned into my mouth while I writhed under him. I climbed higher and higher as his fingers continued. My breaths started coming in pants, and I had to release his mouth and bury my face into his neck. I clutched myself to him, anchoring myself to something permanent as I lost more and more control. The fall wouldn't come.

"I can't." I nearly cried.

"Let go." His fingers shifted and rubbed at just the right angle and I dropped from that cliff with a long, keening moan into his shoulder.

I don't know how I didn't pass out, but when I opened my eyes, Elliot was lifting from me with an intent expression. I couldn't see what was around us since the fire now burned low. He covered the fire pit with the screen, buttoned his shorts, and carried me into the house without stopping.

When we reached his bathroom, he tenderly removed my clothes one piece at a time, followed by his own. All I could do was lean against the counter in this odd sort of daze. He was so beautiful. Lean muscle covered with soft skin and only a smattering of hair on his chest that trailed down below those sexy black boxer briefs he liked to wear. The tattoo I'd wondered about turned out to be an armband with a line of fleur de lis wrapped with heavy bands above and below. It suited him, and I confess it was hot.

He pulled me under the warm spray of the shower and leaned me against the wall. After he soaped us both and washed my hair, he tugged me out of the spray and wrapped me in an enormous towel.

As he reached for another, I opened mine and wrapped it around us both, nuzzling my nose into his neck before I scraped my teeth against that place where his neck met his shoulder. His body shivered against mine, and I smiled. He'd done the same to me the other night. I'd barely been able to stand.

"Elliot," I whispered against his jaw. I caressed the faint stubble on his cheeks. That tiny hint of a beard was crazy hot.

"Hmm?" He stood so ramrod still with the exception of his hands that now grasped my sides almost painfully.

I slid up to my toes and kissed his soft lips. "Make love to me."

His eyebrows popped along with his eyes. "Are you sure?"

I guided him toward the bedroom, pressed him back onto the bed, and tossed the towel away. My knees straddled him, and I planted my hands on either side of his head. Then, I kissed him without holding anything back.

His fingers wound into my hair, and he groaned as he rolled me onto my back. Our lips continued to tangle while our hands roamed. When I reached down and took him into my palm, he pulled my hand up near our heads and entwined our fingers. "If you start doing that, this will be over far sooner than I want it to be."

I lifted my thighs to cradle his hips while he ground against me. Meanwhile, his lips wandered everywhere. My stomach, my breasts, and my neck were all tasted before he settled between my thighs. I gasped at the first kiss to the inside of my leg. I'd only ever had the one sexual partner, and he never would have kissed me below the belly button. My entire body tensed waiting for Elliot's next move. When his tongue touched my clit, I thought I would jump out of my skin.

"I love the way you taste, Maggie."

He settled on his stomach and licked, kissed, and sucked until tears started pouring from my eyes. One of his fingers slipped inside, and my back arched so high I practically sat up on the bed. All it took was a slight scrape of his teeth to push me so far over the edge, I nearly screamed.

"I need you now," I said, grasping his ass as he shifted over me.

"We need a condom."

"I'm on the pill." I lifted up to kiss him, desperate for that connection. "Please, Elliot. I need to feel you inside of me."

He pressed his full weight on top of me and kissed me as he sank inside. His forehead dropped to my shoulder. "God, you feel so good."

I wrapped my legs around him, greedy for every precious inch. I'd never been filled so completely. As we started to rock together, our free hands met and our fingers entwined while we lost ourselves in each other.

When a tear leaked from my eye, his eyebrows drew down in the center. "Am I hurting you?"

"No, I swear you're not. Please don't stop."

That ache I'd fought for the past week was finally assuaged and replaced with this coiling that wound tighter and tighter. My hips shifted of their own accord to meet his. He grasped my ass and changed the angle of his thrusts, making me cry out on the first. My arms wrapped around him tightly, and I buried my face into his shoulder.

"Mags, I want to see you come. Please."

I dropped my head back to the pillow right as he hit that spot—the one that radiated through every nerve fiber and reached all the way to my fingertips. His pace quickened, and he thrust harder until everything in front of me faded away and I shattered into a million tiny pieces.

A sob tore from my chest, but when I finally opened my eyes, Elliot's had involuntarily closed his as he came and collapsed on top of me. When he lifted and tried to roll off, I wrapped my legs around him. "No!"

"You're crying. You told me I wasn't hurting you."

"You weren't. I swear," I said as clearly as I could. "Please don't go."

"Then tell me what's wrong."

"Nothing. It's so stupid. Really. I promise it's nothing." My palms rested on his cheeks as I tried to bring him to me for a kiss.

"Then tell me why you're crying."

"Because it was perfect, okay. It's never been like that— ever."

"Yeah?" His lips curved into such a ridiculously proud expression, I suddenly wanted to slap him silly.

I pinched his side, making him flinch and yelp. "Ouch!"

"Stop looking so smug."

"I'm sorry." He laughed and kissed me soundly. "I can't help it. If it makes you feel better, it was perfect for me too. You're different, Mags. I've never felt this way with another. I've also never been with a woman without a condom until you." His fingers brushed my hair from my face. "I'm falling in love with you."

My heart all but burst from my chest when he said the "L" word. "I'm falling in love with you too."

Chapter 10

"Mommy!" Harper barreled around my office door. I'd barely managed to turn my chair before she jumped into my lap, backpack and all.

"Umph! You're getting awfully big to do that."

Elliot rounded the corner, grinning when he saw Harper. "Hey, Harpoon, be careful. You're going to break her legs one of these days." Harper finally asked him a few days ago what harpoon meant. She hadn't noticed he only called her that when she jumped into a situation with the momentum of an intercontinental ballistic missile.

Two weeks had passed since we first spent the weekend at Elliot's, and him picking up Harper from school on Fridays as well as spending weekends with him had become a tradition. We didn't always kayak on the river. Last weekend, we hiked in the park, which was a lot of fun with the sloping hills and trees. Elliot also made a great guide.

"Hi there."

At the familiar voice, I set Harper on the floor, stood, and moved so I could see Charlie's face rather than only hearing her voice. She held Wyatt secure in her arms and wore a wicked grin that made Elliot turn all sorts of red.

He awkwardly scratched the back of his neck in that way that I adored. "Um, hi."

"Hi, Maggie," she said leaning further around the door. "Hey, Hardy har har."

"Hi, Aunt Charlie."

I stepped up next to Elliot and pinched his side, making him flinch. "How are you?" I asked Charlie.

"I'm great. I simply came in to grab a few files and see if the rumors I've heard are true."

I matched Charlie's stance on the other side of the door frame. "What rumors?"

"Well, first, I heard that my friend Elliot here has been seen a lot around the office. Then Jensen hears at the precinct that the two of you are all hot and heavy."

"Why would the guys talk about us at the precinct?" I honestly didn't understand. I'd never been arrested. I knew a few of them from high school, but other than that. . .

Elliot shrugged. "I know most of them from work."

Charlie pointed straight at Elliot. "He was an EMT. He worked with or knew most of them from accident scenes." I hadn't considered our relationship would be so interesting to so many. The geriatric scene always thrived on who was dating whom and who was getting married. Who knew the Marysville police force was a hotbed of relationship gossip? Charlie snickered an evil sound that let me know something shocking would soon emerge. "You know several of those guys wanted Jensen to hook them up with you?"

"Me?" I squeaked, straightening while Elliot laughed. I peeked behind me to Harper, who spun in dizzying circles in my office chair.

Arms snaked around me from behind and pulled me against a muscled male chest. "Mine," said Elliot from over my shoulder. "Tell your man to make his friends get their own."

Charlie's gaze softened, and she smiled. "Don't worry. He never had any intention of setting up anyone. Could you imagine having to work with someone after a blind date gone bad?" She stepped up beside us, and though Elliot kept one arm wrapped around me, she hugged him. "Is she who you told me about last summer?"

"She is."

"You sure took your time. You do know she's been single for six years?"

I turned my face into his chest, hiding my burning complexion.

"I kept trying to work up the guts to ask her out. It's not the easiest task when you really like someone."

"I know," she said. "We've always given one another a hard time, so when I saw you here, I couldn't resist." As my face cooled, I pulled it from Elliot's chest as Charlie held her next-to-newborn son in my direction. "Maggie, would you hold him for a moment. I can find what I need much faster with two hands."

"Of course." When the baby sank into my embrace, something in my chest melted and oozed through my body. It'd been a while since I'd held one of these. Had I somehow turned off my biological clock? Because it'd never felt like this before.

Charlie didn't hesitate to hurry into her office, but Elliot gave me a strange look. "What's wrong?"

"Nothing."

His chin hitched back a little, but I ignored him and buried my nose in the wisps of hair on Wyatt's head, inhaling that scent that only came with babies.

"I want to see the baby!" Harper skipped up in front of me, so I squatted down so she could see his face.

"You have to speak softly," I said as his eyes blinked a little before he fell back to sleep. Harper's index finger carefully touched Wyatt's arm, stroking up and down.

"He's so cute. When can we get one? I want a baby sister, 'member?"

Elliot's low chuckle vibrated through me, but at that moment, that sound made me want to step on the man's toe rather than jump his bones. He leaned over Harper's shoulder. "We'll see. That's up to your mommy."

I glanced at him as I rose. I hadn't expected him to answer her, but oddly, I didn't mind.

His hand lightly guided my arms in the event I lost my balance. "Why don't I get Harper buckled into the car? Charlie said she'd be back in a minute." I nodded, so he waved his hand for her to follow. "Come on Harmonica."

Charlie stepped out of her office. "Chop chop, Lollipop."

My daughter gave a huge giggle and turned around. "See you soon, Baboon."

I rolled my eyes. "I can't believe you taught her so many of those goodbyes. She loves them, but I don't know them all. I'm dreadfully uncool in her eyes."

"I can send you the link to where I found them." Charlie settled her bag on her shoulder. "Thanks for giving me both hands for a few moments."

"He's very sweet."

"You should change his diapers," said Charlie dryly. "You might change your mind."

I gave his fine baby locks one more casual sniff before I returned him to his mother.

"That smell is addicting, isn't it?" She leaned back against my door frame, watching me for a few moments before she took in a quick breath. "I don't want this to be awkward, but I did the same thing with Brandon and Jena." I opened my mouth, but Charlie held up a finger. "It's just that both of you are my friends, and I don't want either of you to get hurt. So I'm going to tell you the same thing I'm going to tell Elliot about you. You break his heart, I'll kick your ass."

An incredulous bark burst from me, but I knew better than to question her seriousness. I remember Jena mentioning the threat when she'd started dating Charlie's brother, Brandon. "I have no intention of hurting him."

"Good. I better get back to Jensen. He's at Starlight waiting for me. Thanks again."

I called out a "bye" as she headed toward the door. I grabbed my purse and phone and met Elliot at the car. When we entered Gram's house, her friend Amy Louise sat with her on the sofa while they both crocheted.

"Oh, good," said Gram. "I need to speak to you. Why don't we sit on the back porch?"

With a look at Amy Louise then Elliot behind me, I moved my mouth a couple of times, but Elliot pushed me forward. "We'll be fine. See what your grandmother wants."

As soon as I stepped onto the porch, Gram sat in one of the wicker chairs. "I told Amy Louise she could move into the extra bedroom."

"What?" I'd been mid-step when Gram spoke and halted. She certainly hadn't beat around the bush, and my jaw had surely hit the floor with a heavy thud. "I know it's your house, but doesn't my opinion matter? I mean, I've lived here for over six years."

"Of course I care about your feelings, but I want you to look at this from my point of view. You're getting rather serious with that boy—"

"Elliot."

"Yes, him. And I don't doubt that he'll ask you to move in sooner rather than later. Meanwhile, Amy Louise's husband controlled the finances and did a shit job of it. Her house needs to be sold, and the IRS will likely claim it all. It looks as though the only money she'll keep is the life insurance, and that's because, thankfully, the idiot didn't put it in his will. If he had, the IRS may have claimed that too. Anyhow, she was distraught because she would need to move in with her son. Her daughter-in-law was already objecting, and Amy Louise doesn't want to leave Marysville."

"Gram—"

"I'm not finished, Margaret."

I sat down and crossed my legs. "Okay, shoot."

"I don't want you to alter your plans because of me, and Amy Louise needs a place to live. She's fifteen years younger and doesn't mind that I might need her help from time to time. When I'm back on my feet, I can still walk to school to pick up Harper or Amy Louise can drive me if it's raining. But you would be free to follow your heart. You can move in with Elliot when you want as well as marry him without feeling guilty about leaving me behind."

She was making plans in advance to free me of my obligation to her. I really didn't know how to feel about that. "I don't know what to say, Gram." Why did I find it all so. . . disconcerting? I didn't dislike Amy Louise, but I hadn't planned on living with her either.

Gram took a big breath and clasped her hands in her lap. "She needs to move soon, so we planned next weekend. It'll give you an opportunity to talk to Elliot and become accustomed to the idea. We can discuss it more on Monday night. Also, Harper and I had a talk last night. She loves going to Elliot's, but I promised we'd make cookies this weekend so the two of you can have some time alone."

What? "Elliot has no problems spending time with Harper." My voice was defensive, but Gram had this way of making plans she thought were best. Today's were more than I could fathom in one sitting.

"All couples need time alone. I love how he takes care of Harper. She's needed a father for a long time but don't assume he doesn't want one-on-one time with you. Even married parents should have a date night once in a while."

I stood and strode inside. "Harper!"

Her footsteps pounded down the stairs until she stopped at the bottom. "What's wrong, Mommy?"

"You don't want to go to Elliot's this weekend?"

"Gram promised we'd make cookies. Is that okay?"

Elliot's eyebrows drew toward the middle when I glanced at him over her head, but I looked down at Harper, her little eyes wide. "Yes, it's okay. I was surprised is all. I know how much you love Elliot's."

"But I can go next weekend, can't I? If I don't go today, I can always go later."

"Of course, you can," he said, tugging on one of her braids. He glanced at me. "Do you want to stay here instead?"

"The two of you should still go." Gram walked over to the sofa and took her usual spot. "Harper will be fine with us. You two have a good time."

I pointed up the stairs. "I'll go get my things."

"What dress are you gonna wear for the wedding?" When I looked down, Harper peered up at me, her little head tilted. "Can I pick it out?"

"Well, yeah. You always choose my dress." I held out my hand. "Let's go."

After she chose my navy, lace cocktail dress, I packed it with my silver pumps, grabbed my makeup and jewelry, and joined everyone downstairs. I kissed Harper and hugged her tight before Elliot and I got into my car.

"Can we talk when we get to the house?" I pulled away from the curb and turned the next right, headed toward the forest's edge.

"I just want to be sure you're okay."

"I am. I promise. Harper will be fine. My grandmother simply threw me for a loop."

The drive to Elliot's never took more than five minutes. Once Elliot hung my dress in the closet and set my bag on the floor, he pulled me into his arms and propped his chin on my head. "Why don't we change, pour you a glass of wine, and go sit on the swing? I think we do some of our best talking out there, among other things."

I smiled and buried my nose into his chest. Although his work polo still held the faint smell of his cologne, it carried more of the scent of his office. Changing was a good idea.

"Sounds good," I said. "You smell like the clinic."

He lifted his top and gave it a whiff. "I can't have that." He laughed and pulled it off, throwing it in the hamper.

I set my palm over his heart and let it slide over his glorious pecs. He grabbed my wrist with a smile. "You start touching me, and we won't be talking." I bit my bottom lip and reached for his belt. We could talk after.

⚯

Elliot sat in the swing, and when I joined him, he kept it steady so I wouldn't spill my wine. This evening, I sat on the opposite side, facing him, with my knees lifted and my feet on the cushion.

One at a time, he pulled my feet into his lap and began rubbing them. The evenings were cooler than a few weeks ago, but October had a way of doing that. Rather than wearing short-sleeves, Elliot wore a long-sleeve grey t-shirt and a pair of sweat pants while I wore a comfy thermal nightgown and carried a chunky knit blanket.

I propped my elbow on the back of the swing and rested my head against my hand, the afghan covering most of my legs. "Gram has invited Amy Louise to move in."

He frowned and his hand stilled for a moment. "She didn't speak to you first?"

I swallowed my first sip of wine with a sigh. "No, but it's her house. Is it unreasonable to think she should've asked me?"

He pivoted some more to face me. "I don't think so. You've lived there for six years now, right?"

"Yes, since not long before Harper was born."

"And you helped pay off her mortgage."

"I did, but I've never had to pay rent, per se. I merely helped out with the bills and the upkeep."

His fingernails trailed up and down the top of the foot he had massaged. "That's not much different than rent. Did she give you any idea of her reason for not consulting you?"

I groaned and drew my hand over my face. "She doesn't want me to feel obligated to her. This way, if you ask Harper and I to move in with you, I don't feel as though I'm abandoning her."

"Oh," he said softly. "I did wonder if one day I would need to move in with you. The only problem with your house is that we never do more than sleep."

My eyebrows shot up without thought. "Are you so sex deprived?"

"No," he drawled, "but if we lived there, would you want to have sex in your grandmother's house?"

"This is a ridiculous conversation." I sipped my wine and nudged his leg. "Gram has ensured we wouldn't live there anyway."

"So why didn't Harper come this weekend?"

"Because Gram felt we should have time to ourselves."

His fingers inched further under the blanket and caressed the side of my knee, giving me goosebumps that I struggled to ignore. "Your daughter is amazing, but I won't object having you to myself on occasion." He watched me for a moment while his fingers continued to skim along my leg. "Have you ever spent the night away from her?"

"Once, when she had a sleepover at Mei's." I glanced down into what was left of my merlot. We'd just made love, and his touches would soon have me straddling him if he didn't stop. "When have you thought about us moving in?" I waved my hand circles, urging him to elaborate. "Like considered it, you know. Not that we need to do it right now."

He grinned and grasped my calf, squeezing. "I knew what you meant. Relax." He took a sip of his beer and rested it on his knee. "I've thought about it a lot. More and more since you and Harper first stayed the weekend. We'd need to get her furniture. She can't live in that tent—even if she'd love it. I never saw the point in furnishing rooms I never used so I never bothered. You won't be displacing anything of mine."

I shook my head and held up my hand, palm out. "I don't want you to take us in tomorrow because my grandmother expects it to happen one day."

He set his beer on the ground, then took my wine glass and did the same. When he crawled over me, I sank down onto the seat cushion and pulled the blanket over my face.

"No, you're not hiding from me." He drew the cover down and slipped it over us both. His index finger trailed from the base of my neck to the first fastened button of my thermal gown. He released it and moved to the second. "I've wanted to make love to you on this swing since you first sat out here with me."

After he exposed my chest, he rucked my skirt up to my waist. "God, I love that you're not wearing panties."

I lay on Elliot's chest while I blearily watched the flickering lights from the fireflies across the water. One of his hands toyed with my hair, combing it from my temple carefully. Despite our recent activities, he kept those goosebumps ever present down my spine. His other palm rested on my thigh where I straddled his hips.

"I love you," he whispered against the top of my head.

Something in my chest shattered and flooded my heart. When had my feelings deepened to love? I had no idea. I only knew that my heart seemed swollen from how strong my feelings were.

I turned my head far enough to kiss his chest. "I love you too."

"Move in with me."

I inhaled and lifted so I could see his face. "Elliot—"

"Not because your grandmother expects it, but because you want to be with me. I want it all with you, Mags. I want to marry you, I want to adopt Harper and be her father, and I hope you might let me help make a little brother or sister for her one day. I know we haven't been seeing each other for long, but I'm also not asking for everything right now—just for you to want to be with me."

"Yes," I said softly, a tear forging a wet trail down my cheek to drop to his chest.

"Yes?" The smile he wore appeared so young and carefree.

"Yes." Our laughter drowned out the crickets until I claimed his lips with mine. We would've made love on the swing again if a crack of thunder hadn't preceded a deluge of rain that sent us scurrying into the house for Elliot's warm king-sized bed.

Chapter 11

I took a sip of my wine and propped the glass on the edge of the bathtub. What an insane day! I closed my eyes and sank further into the warm water, letting it soothe my frazzled nerves. Thank the Lord for the large, old-fashioned tub in Elliot's master bathroom—or as of three weeks ago, our bathroom.

When I arrived home from the Leonard wedding—or what was supposed to be the Leonard wedding—to an empty house, I opened a bottle of wine and took it and a glass to the bathroom to soak away the remainder of the day, which I fully intended to do.

"Well, hello there." I allowed my aching head to drop to the side and cracked one eye open. Elliot leaned against the wall with an enormous grin. "This is a view I could certainly get used to."

I turned the hot water on with my toe and let it run for a second, bringing the temperature up a notch. "Where did you two go?"

He grabbed my vanity seat and pulled it beside the tub. "I took Harper to the fitness center."

My eyes opened the rest of the way. "To the fitness center?"

"Don't worry. I'm not turning her into one of those bodybuilding bikini models."

"Ha, ha," I said before I took another sip of my wine.

He leaned over and kissed my forehead. "Do you remember when Harper said she hated volleyball?"

"Yes, and you promised to help her." I patted the bubbles and arranged them in front of me. "Is that what the two of you did?"

"We used the racket ball court, so when she served, the ball would bounce back. Sometimes, if you're lucky, you can hit it when it returns. She can now serve, and I got her hitting the ball when I toss it to her."

"That's great," I said brushing a loose chunk of hair behind my ear. "Where is she now?"

"Taking a bath."

I nodded and took a gulp of my wine.

Elliot lifted his eyebrows with a slight tilt of his head. "How was the wedding?"

"Didn't happen." I chased the last gulp with another.

"Seriously?"

"Yup! Apparently, all hell broke loose at the bridal breakfast, and I missed it."

His eyebrows drew together. "But as far as I know, Charlie has never worked anything like that. Were you supposed to cover this one?"

"No, the contract only required us to arrange it." I took another sip and held out my glass for Elliot to refill. "The bottle is on the floor. Please?"

He uncorked and poured before he handed the glass back to me. "So what happened at the breakfast?"

"Well!" I took the glass and waved it along with my free hand. "It seems the groom was schtupping one of the bridesmaids, and she believed up until that morning that he would call off the wedding and carry her off into the sunset."

"Oh, no," he said in a groan.

"Oh, yes. So, this morning, when she realized he planned to go through with the wedding, she announced to all and sundry, including her own mother, who was best friends with the mother of the bride, her various escapades with the groom— in vivid detail. I arrived shortly after since the breakfast, the ceremony, and the reception were all at The Coastal."

"That swanky hotel down on the lake?"

"The very one," I drawled. I took a sip and swallowed. "Anyway, the fit had hit the shan not long before I arrived, the bride had high-tailed it—not that I blame her—and the groom and the parents refused to make the embarrassing announcement. That was left to me."

He leaned against his thighs with a grimace. "What did you do?"

"There wasn't much I could do but apologize and explain that due to unforeseen circumstances no wedding would occur. Then I offered for everyone to go to the ballroom and enjoy the reception. The bride's parents were furious at that, but why let all that food go to waste?" I sat up and pointed at him. "You see, they assumed they wouldn't be required to pay since the wedding didn't happen."

Elliot began laughing, and I shot him a withering glare. "I'm sorry," he said between chuckles. "Did they think the company would simply eat the cost?"

"Who knows?" I took another drink. After a moment, I turned to catch him not looking at my face, but down lower. "Hey!" I splashed him, making him sputter. "I'm telling you about my shit day at work, and you're staring at my tits?"

"I wasn't at first, but you sat up, and they're so pretty all wet and covered in bubbles."

I sank back into the water and closed my eyes.

"Did you call anyone?"

"Jena has a huge wedding in Charleston today, and Ellie was off. Jacob's tooth popped through a few days ago, so he's better. I just didn't want to bug her on her free day so I called Charlie."

"What did she say?"

"You mean after she cackled hysterically at the absurdity of it all?" I shook my head and propped my glass against the edge of the tub once again. "She's coming in with Wyatt first thing Monday morning to work on billing. She plans on calling them then. They signed a contract. Deposits for venues cannot be refunded and food cannot be unbought. They're financially responsible. If they refuse to pay in ninety days, it goes to collection."

"Ouch." He took my wine and set it on the floor with a clink. "I need to mention something to you, and I need you sober."

"I can't handle bad news, Elliot." My voice was whiny and pathetic, but at least I knew my own limits.

"It's not bad news, sweetheart." He reached into the water and took my hand. "After we practiced volley ball, I took Harper to the pet supply store for some duck food, and we went to the pond."

"I bet she loved that."

He smiled in this adorable way that made me reach up and give him a quick kiss. "She did. She had a great time. Anyway, while we fed the ducks, she asked me if I could visit her class and talk about my job. Apparently, all the kids are having their dads do it."

"She asked you?" I sat up and bent my legs, clutching them to my chest with my free arm. "I signed up for the moms' event. If you're not okay with it, I can talk to her."

"No, I want to." His hand squeezed mine. "Maggie, she asked me if I wanted to be her daddy. I couldn't tell her that I needed to speak to you first, so I told her the truth."

I lifted my eyebrows. He'd said he'd wanted to adopt Harper but did he say that to her?

"We sat on the bench, and I explained that if she wanted me to be her dad, that I could adopt her. I told her I'd be honored to be her father because she's a great little girl."

"What'd she say?"

"She said yes." He let out a shuddering breath and clasped both hands around my one. "I know you wanted to be sure about everything, but I'm certain about this—about you. I hope you aren't upset with me for speaking to her without your go-ahead."

"No," I said breathing out. "If you'd told her to wait, she would've taken it as a rejection. You did exactly what you should've done. I asked to wait because I didn't want you to adopt her and regret it down the line."

"Hey." He tipped my chin up. "I'm not that dickhead Sawyer. I'm not going to run away." Without pausing, he stood, whipped off his shirt and shorts, and stepped into the bathtub. He hadn't even removed his boxer briefs. When he sat down, the water rose and trickled down the overflow drain. "Come here."

I scooted toward him, and he embraced me, drawing me so close I had to wrap my legs around his waist. "I can't believe you're still in your underwear."

"I didn't want you to think I was jumping in for any other reason but to talk. Maybe another time but not right now."

One side of my lips tugged upward, unable to resist his cheeky add-on. "I know you're not Sawyer."

"We moved in together quickly, but I've told you that I'm serious about us. I want it all with you."

"And I believe you," I said. He had to understand that I thought him nothing like Sawyer.

"Good, because I meant it; however, as much as I want it all for us, I don't want to rush any more than we already have. I'm loving every part of being with you." He pressed a kiss to my lips then my shoulder. "Do you have an attorney? We're going to need one to file the paperwork."

I scrunched my nose and relaxed into his lap. "I went to legal aid after Harper was born to make up a will. I wanted Gram to have custody if something happened to me. Without any other family, she would've gone to foster care." I scraped my teeth along my bottom lip. "I really should change that and put you as her guardian. Gram would struggle keeping up with Harper on her own for long term."

"I have a local attorney I used to help get my clearances to renovate this house. I'll check with her on Monday and see if she can draw up the paperwork or refer us to someone else." He grinned that wicked one I loved so much. "Now that we've settled matters, turn around and I'll scrub your back."

The slight scratch of the loofah between my shoulder blades made me melt and lean my forehead against the side of the tub. After, Elliot removed his underwear and soaped up quickly before he tugged me back to lie against his chest.

"This is nice," I said.

"Mmmm."

I chuckled at Elliot's sleepy response near my ear. My eyes drifted closed, but I didn't fall asleep. Instead, my muscles slowly turned to limp noodles, especially with Elliot rubbing my lower back the way he was.

"Mommy?"

My eyes shot open, and I frantically surveyed the room. "What's up, Harp?"

"Whatcha doin'?"

Elliot's chest shook, and he kissed the side of my neck. "She's in the bedroom. We'll never have time to get dressed. At least you drained and refilled the bubble bath so we're covered."

"Taking a bath," I called, glancing over my shoulder at Elliot, who still enjoyed this entirely too much. Before I could yell to wait where she was, her little head peeked around the corner.

"Hey, Harpoon."

"You're takin' a bath with Daddy?" Her eyes darted back and forth between me and Elliot. "Lu said her mommy and daddy sleep in the same bed like you do." Her eyes shifted to my bare shoulders and the floor where Elliot's soaked boxer briefs lay in a ball. "Do mommies and daddies see each other nekkid?"

Something resembling a squeak escaped while Elliot's chest began shaking even harder. My fingers slipped under the water and pinched his side. He hissed and pinched me back.

"We do." I suppose I had to be honest about it. "But it's not something you need to talk about with Lu or anyone else at school. Okay?"

"Okay. Did Daddy tell you I can call him Daddy? He's going to come to school for Daddy day. I'll have a daddy just like everyone else."

"Yes, Sweet Pea. He did." I swallowed hard. "I think he'll be more awesome than all the other daddies there. Don't you?"

Harper nodded, and I jumped on the brief silence. "Did you put your dirty clothes in the basket or are they on the bathroom floor?"

Her little body stiffened. She didn't need to say a word for me to know the answer.

"Go do that and turn on the TV in the living room. Elliot and I will be out in a few minutes."

"But I'm hungry."

"Go grab a banana, and Mommy and I will decide about dinner while we get dressed. Does that work?"

Without a word, she raced out of the room and my head dropped back on his shoulder. "Do mommies and daddies see each other naked? I could've gone years without answering that one."

"I think this is my fault. You told her to knock when the door was closed. I think I forgot to shut it behind me when I came in, but in all fairness, I didn't think you'd be all inviting and lure me into this bath."

"Inviting?"

"Yeah, inviting." He rubbed the erection we'd been ignoring against my rear.

I laughed while I stood, grabbed my towel from the hook, and stepped out onto the mat. "One day, I'll have to show you what inviting really looks like."

He stood dripping wet, his cock pointing like an arrow in my direction. "You promise." He followed, and before I could get escape, wrapped his arms around me from behind.

"Argh! You're going to get my towel soaked." I threw my towel over his head and grabbed another from the basket while scurrying for the bedroom.

The door was open so I closed it long enough to throw on some leggings and a sweater. We'd probably have a lazy evening, and I preferred to be comfortable.

"Pizza from Giuseppe's?" he asked. "We can all walk down and pick it up."

"Sounds good to me."

That evening, I rolled over in Elliot's arms to face him. One thing I'd learned since moving in was that he slept like the dead, but he could wake at any hour of the morning without being crabby about it.

Had it only been two short months? The time had passed so quickly! One September day, he was at the house picking up Gram in the ambulance for her broken hip, and the next, November had arrived, we were living with him, and he wanted to adopt Harper.

Somehow, he'd sneaked into my well-guarded heart and filled it until it was overflowing. He made a point of saying he was nothing like Sawyer, which was so true. I never could've loved Sawyer as much as Elliot. I still didn't understand how I'd once thought Sawyer my entire world—young love perhaps?

His eyes slowly fluttered open, and he frowned. "What's wrong?"

"Nothing. I'm just thinking."

He rolled to his back and pulled me over until my head rested on his shoulder. "Go to sleep." An enormous sighed exhale made me smile. "Love you."

"I love you too." And I meant it. A part of me had been hesitant about moving too quickly, but something had changed. I didn't know when it had, but all I now knew was that I'd marry him tomorrow if he asked.

I closed my eyes and sank further into the covers. Tomorrow morning, he'd never remember waking. He'd probably been half-asleep when he first blinked those beautiful hazel eyes—not that it mattered. He was still trying to take care of me, even while he slept.

Chapter 12

I looked out at the water then back at the bridge that seemed to stretch into forever. When Elliot mentioned the possibility of spending Thanksgiving in Louisiana with his parents, a part of me wanted to hunker down and insist on spending the holiday with Gram, but that's what I always did, play it safe. I couldn't hide from his parents forever, could I?

So, here I was in a rental car while Elliot drove us across Lake Pontchartrain. We'd flown into the airport in New Orleans, which was certainly a new experience for myself and Harper. Neither of us had ever so much as stepped on an airplane before this morning, but we hadn't had the time to drive. Instead, Elliot had informed the airline of Harper's allergy, so they allowed us to board early to wipe down our seats and tray tables. We sat in the first set of seats, and the flight attendants ensured the people around us weren't snacking on nuts. Fortunately, everyone had been extremely kind about any inconvenience they may have felt.

I'd even brought a bag full of snacks for her as well as her own blanket. For a bit of extra protection, I'd also given her an antihistamine and brought more as well as two epi-pens to be on the safe side.

With the flight done, we only had to meet Elliot's parents. Between the humidity and my nerves, I was about to sweat through my pale grey t-shirt. Leave it to me to wear one of the most noticeable colors to sweat through! What would his mother do if I went to shake her hand and left a slick of sweat?

"You're too quiet."

"I'm freaking nervous." I wiped my palms up and down my thighs in a vain attempt to dry them.

He chuckled and reached over to take my hand. "Relax. My parents don't bite. When I told Mom about Harper's allergy, she scoured the house from top to bottom and gave the neighbor every nut product in the kitchen to be on the safe side. You have nothing to worry about."

"I hope she gets them all back after we leave. She didn't have to give away food."

"My mom would never forgive herself if something happened. Don't worry about it. We can send her a bunch by online shopping when we get home." He squeezed my hand and glanced in the rearview mirror at Harper. "How are you doing, Harmonica?"

"I need to pee."

I peered over my shoulder. "Unfortunately, we can't stop here. I don't think it will be much longer."

"Can you hold it?" Elliot glanced into the rearview again. "It's not too much farther, but tell me if it's an emergency."

Once we got off that interminable bridge, the drive wasn't far before we pulled onto a street lined with massive old oaks, their Spanish moss hanging like long, grey tresses of hair over the road. The homes were small, but by the style, had to have been here for decades if not longer.

Finally, Elliot pulled into the driveway in front of a narrow, powder blue home with white trim. Baskets hung between the white beams on the front porch, laden with purple and yellow pansies winking in the mid-day sun. A single swing hung to one side, inviting someone to sit and rock the evening away.

Elliot leaned over and kissed me with a smile before he got out. He opened Harper's door, then walked around to mine since I was procrastinating while I tried to pull my shit together. When I stood and looked at the house again, an older woman stood on the porch, a welcoming smile upon her face. "You're early."

"Traffic wasn't too bad coming out of New Orleans." Harper tugged on Elliot's arm. "Mom, Harper needs to use the bathroom in a bad way. Can you show her where it is while Maggie and I get the bags?"

"Well, of course." She waved Harper over. "Come on, sweetheart. Let's get you inside before you can't hold it anymore." Much to my shock, my normally shy daughter ran inside without Elliot or I nudging her in the woman's direction.

"I guess if someone wants to kidnap her, they need to make the attempt while she really needs to pee," I said softly.

Elliot handed me Harper's backpack from the backseat and grabbed the two small carry-on suitcases from the trunk. He even ducked into the front seat and handed me the large leather tote bag I'd brought in place of a purse. He managed to hold one of those carry-ons under his arm while he held the other in his hand, leaving one hand free to grab mine. "Come on."

"Elliot, wait," I said as I grabbed his arm. "Did you tell her I'm Black?"

"No, I didn't." I opened my mouth but he set down a bag and cradled my face in his hands. "I didn't tell her, because she won't care." He pressed a hard kiss to my lips. "Now, come meet my parents."

By the time we reached the porch, his mother was back outside. "We're so glad y'all could come. Why don't we get you inside and those bags in your rooms?" Elliot kissed his mother's cheek, and before I could say "hello," she wrapped her arms around me.

"I'm so happy to finally meet you."

As soon as I stepped into the small but homey living room, the smells of pumpkin pie and cinnamon overwhelmed.

"You bought new furniture," said Elliot.

"Oh, it was past time. Your father had finally worn a hole in the seat of that ancient recliner, and you remember how the sofa springs creaked something fierce. Anyway, we found that couch down the road on clearance. Your dad made the coffee table, sofa table, and shelves to match it for me. I got the idea off that Pinterest." Her eyes honed in on me. "Do you ever go on there? They have some wonderful ideas."

I couldn't prevent one side of my lips lifting. "I use Pinterest a lot. My clients will also find ideas on there and bring them to me. We can't always make it the exact same, but we can usually come close."

His mother nodded and opened a door. "Harper can stay in here."

I peeked around the doorframe, and my eyes surely bugged at the sight of Elliot's childhood room. Athletics trophies lined shelves over a chest of drawers on one side, a twin bed so small that I could imagine his feet hanging over the footboard ran the length of the opposite wall, and a desk with a bulletin board sat beside it. There wasn't much space, but it was comfortable.

Unable to resist, I slipped past and bent over the desk to look at the pictures tacked onto the board. I could make him out in a few, but one was of the offensive line at a football game. "Where are you?" I peered back over my shoulder.

"Elliot was the quarterback," said his mom proudly.

When I leaned over further, I spotted Elliot's tell-tale grin under the helmet as he waited for the center to hike the ball. "And did you date the head cheerleader?" I couldn't resist!

He reddened and did that adorable, awkward scratch to the back of his neck. "No, I dated the valedictorian." I laughed and poked him in the side.

"Mommy?"

"Hey, Harp, this is your room. What do you think? It was Elliot's when he was your age." I didn't know what Elliot had told his mom about Harper, and I didn't want to start that discussion with my daughter in the room.

"Really?"

"Yep!" He picked her up under her arms and swung her around before putting her feet back on the floor. "Is that okay?"

She nodded while she surveyed the room. Her demeanor was quieter than usual, but she was rarely outgoing with new people. I always thought it was odd how quickly she took to Giuseppe.

"Why don't I show you where you're going to sleep?" His mother led us through the kitchen to a glassed-in back porch where an air mattress was made up on the floor as well as a hammock on the other side. "I hope this will do. I'm afraid the house isn't very large."

"It's great, Mrs. Martin." I smiled and set down my bag. The house was clean and welcoming. I didn't require a fancy guest room to be happy.

"Thanks, Mom."

"Daddy?"

"Yes, Harpsichord?"

"Can I play with the games in your room?" As she spoke, her head tilted in that shy way that made me want to hold her close.

"Sure, if you want, we can get a few of them out later and play them at the kitchen table."

Harper hopped forward and jumped at Elliot. He caught her easily and lifted her for a kiss to her cheek before setting her back down. After she'd disappeared back into the house, Mrs. Martin sighed with a smile. "She's a sweet little girl."

"She's incredible." Elliot grabbed me around the waist. "Just like her mom." My heart went pitter-patter while I found my feet inordinately interesting.

"I'll let you get settled. If you want to lie down, lower the blinds. The room won't be completely dark, but it will dim it some."

"Thanks, Mom."

"Thank you, Mrs. Martin."

As soon as his mother left the room, he laughed and pulled me into his arms. "Relax."

I shook my head while I inhaled what remained of his cologne. I was meeting the man's mother. I needed all the comfort I could get.

Thanksgiving dinner had been delicious. Mrs. Martin had prepared all the usuals: turkey, stuffing, sweet potatoes, and several vegetable casseroles. She'd even made the desserts herself, down to the crust, which Elliot claimed she did every year.

His father was a lot like Elliot—tall, hazel-eyed, and with a laid-back sense of humor that kept me from getting as nervous as the day before. He also took to Harper quickly. My usually shy child even called him Grandpa by the end of the day.

Harper and I helped Mrs. Martin cook. My daughter had an amazing time since she loved to be in the kitchen. Between all the food, Elliot's old games, and cooking, Harper fell asleep on the sofa rather early during the football game.

"I'll put her in bed," whispered Elliot.

While he carried her from the living room, I stayed relaxed in the corner of the sofa. Mrs. Martin had excused herself to the kitchen a few moments before. I'd tried to help her with dishes, but the woman had staunchly refused, shooing me back to the living room.

"I was beginning to think I'd never see him settle down." My eyes widened when Mr. Martin—Robert, chuckled and shook his head. "You're the first woman he's ever brought home. His mother is extremely relieved. She's always wanted grandchildren." After he checked the door to the kitchen, he reached over and patted my hand. "My wife, like you and your daughter, isn't the most outgoing, so know she's happy you and Elliot are together. She simply needs to get to know you."

Elliot strode back in, bent over, and kissed me on the forehead. "I'm going to grab a beer. Do you want a glass of wine?"

"No, I'm fine. Thanks."

He disappeared into the kitchen with his mother while I sort of blankly stared at the television. Next thing I knew, arms slipped around me and lifted me from the sofa. "Mags?"

"Mmm?"

"Enjoying your tryptophan coma?" His chest shook as he chuckled near my ear.

"I'm awake. You can put me down."

"That's okay. I'm rather enjoying myself."

He finally set me down when we were on the porch. His mouth covered mine and kissed me deeply before I pressed him back. "Let me get ready for bed."

I picked up my thermal night gown and changed in the bathroom after I brushed my teeth. When I returned, Elliot lifted the blankets on the air mattress. I wasn't sure if his mother had intended for us to share, but we'd never asked.

One of his hands snaked under the skirt of the nightgown and pulled me back flush to him. "You're so warm, but why did you have to wear panties?"

"We're in your parents' house?" I hissed quietly.

"So?"

His fingers crept under the elastic and dipped between my legs, finding that sensitive place that could make me writhe. His opposite hand squeezed my breast and sent a jolt straight to my core.

"Elliot, we can't."

"Why? No one will know. You'll have to be quiet, though. You're usually not very good at that part." I gasped when his finger entered me and the heel of his hand rubbed my clit just so. "Shh," he laughed near my ear. "Do you want me?" The words were whispered ever so softly.

"God, yes," I groaned.

My panties were slipped off before he drew me back against his bare body. He shifted one leg forward almost rolling me to my stomach.

"Elliot?"

"Be quiet," he whispered as he easily filled me in one long, gratifying slide. His teeth sank into my shoulder while I pressed my face into my pillow and attempted to smother my groan. The hum of my body increased its pitch with every long stroke and caress.

I whimpered and moaned into the pillow while he murmured into my neck. Not every word was intelligible, but it was obvious they were words of praise, describing how warm and tight I was and how turned on I'd made him.

When his fingers reached around and found my clit, his other hand clamped over my mouth. I'd tried to keep quiet, but he had to know when he pinched that small bit of flesh that I'd lose my mind.

My skin continued to tingle even after he collapsed on top of me. "If your parents heard me, I'm going to be horrified."

"The kitchen and Harper's room are between us. I doubt the sound carried so well. Besides, it's not like we have a headboard to bang against the wall here."

"Your mother is going to hate me. I'm going to be the slut who had sex with her son in her house."

He laughed into my neck. "She actually loves you and adores Harper. She asked me when I was going to propose and had we discussed children. She's got grandbaby fever. She does want Harper to call her grandma though."

I groaned and grabbed my panties from the floor beside the air mattress. "Put your underwear back on. If they come in and we're naked, I'll die of embarrassment."

Once we cuddled back together, he kissed my neck. "I wasn't trying to embarrass you. I'm simply happy and wanted to be with you."

I rolled over and wrapped myself around him. "I know. I'm not really mad, but don't be shocked if my face is crimson for the rest of our stay."

"I love you."

"I love you too."

Chapter 13

As embarrassed as I'd been when we went to bed on Thanksgiving, my discomfort was nothing to when I entered the kitchen the following morning. Mrs. Martin had been humming while she brewed coffee but stopped when my footstep caused a floor board to creak. Her eyes flitted to the hickey Elliot had left on my neck. She'd giggled and wished me good morning while I'd cursed at not bringing a scarf with me.

"Maggie!" I startled and attempted to stifle the heat that rose to my cheeks. "Whatever you're thinking about, I'm not sure I want to know," said Charlie, snickering. "Sorry, but I've said your name three times without an answer."

"My mind wandered."

"Obviously. You must have had a good trip." Charlie plopped down into the chair across from my desk. "I've always wondered what Elliot's parents are like."

"Very kind and humble. By the time we left, Harper was calling them grandma and grandpa."

"That's really great." Charlie smiled with a slightly tilted head. "One can never have too many grandparents, and since she's only had your grandmother, now she gets a bit more spoiling."

"I suppose that's true. I'd never considered it that way."

A sudden cry filled the room from the baby monitor in Charlie's hand. "And he finally wakes up. I had no idea when I put him down to work on the books that he'd sleep for four hours. If I'd been home I would've taken a long nap." She stood and turned off the monitor. "I better change him and get him fed so we can go home."

"Drive safely," I said to Charlie's wave as she walked into the hall.

I sighed and looked back at my computer screen. We'd been back from Louisiana for a little over a week, and I still managed to daydream about that night. I suppose there was something crazy hot about clandestinely making love in his parents' house while attempting with everything in you not to give away what you were doing.

My cell phone buzzed, drawing my attention away from the computer. Gram's name and picture filled the screen when I turned it over, so I touched the glass to answer. "Hi, Gram."

"I'm sorry to interrupt, but I need you to stop by the house. Can you leave early?"

I frowned while I glanced at the time on the computer. I didn't have any more appointments for the day, but I still needed to pick up Harper in thirty minutes. "Let me pick up Harp, and I'll be right over."

"Can't Elliot do that?"

"I'll have to see if I can catch him. He had clients all day last I heard from him." That was this morning when we broke out some equipment he kept in storage and exercised before Harper woke up. He could've had a cancellation, but I couldn't bank on that.

"Please call him and find out. If not, see if Mei can do it."

My stomach tightened while I reached down for my purse. "Gram, what's going on?"

"You'll see when you get here."

I hit end and walked out of my office. When I poked my face into Jena's, her blonde head lifted from whatever she was writing.

"I need to leave. I don't know what's going on, but Gram is insistent. You know what happened the last time she called me at work."

Jena straightened and set down her pen. "Of course. Please let us know if you need anything."

"Thanks, I will."

As soon as I was out the door, I called Elliot's number, which he answered on the first ring. "Hello, beautiful."

I clicked my key to unlock the car. "I need you to pick up Harper if you can."

"What's wrong?" His voice adopted a more intimate tone than when he'd answered.

"I'm not sure. Gram called me a little while ago and insisted I come by the house. She wouldn't say why and said someone else had to pick up Harper. I have this weird feeling she doesn't want Harper there for some reason."

"I've got it covered. Text me when you know what's going on or else I'll worry."

"I'll try. Love you."

"I love you too." His side of the line clicked so I tossed my phone on the passenger seat and started the car. I parked along the street behind the house since Amy Louise's car now usually occupied the garage. Once I let myself into the backyard, I climbed the steps Elliot and I built on the deck and let myself into the house.

"Gram! I'm here. What's so. . ." My stride along with my words came to a sudden halt at the sight of two people I never thought I'd see again sitting in my grandmother's living room. My heart began to race. I opened my mouth, but nothing came out.

The couple stood as did Gram, who'd been sitting in a chair opposite them. "Maggie, you remember Mr. and Mrs. Crawford, don't you?"

I nodded and cleared my throat harshly. "Of course." Damn, my voice was still hoarse.

Mrs. Crawford wrung her hands in front of her. She looked older of course, but she also appeared exhausted—worn. "How are you?" Her fingers lightly brushed a tendril of ginger-colored hair, which was a shade or two lighter than Harper's, from her cheek.

"I'm good, thanks." I swallowed as hard as I could. Perhaps that would dislodge the vomit or whatever else was stinging the back of my throat. "I hope both of you have been well."

Her lip quivered, and she peered over to her husband. He opened his jacket and pulled out a folded piece of paper. "I don't know a better way of saying this, so I'm going to come right out with it. Sawyer was killed on Thanksgiving in a drunk driving accident."

I stepped down from the kitchen and set my hand on the back of the nearest chair. "I'm very sorry to hear that."

His father didn't really acknowledge my condolences but trained his eyes on that folded paper still in his hands. "Sawyer changed after the two of you broke up. He finished his degree, but he was angry and drank. I'm afraid the accident that took his life was his own fault. We're incredibly thankful no one else was killed because of his drunkenness."

"He ran off the road into a tree," said Gram softly.

I nodded, though I couldn't do more than stare at the two people in front of me. Mrs. Crawford sat and dabbed her eyes with a tissue. A box of Gram's preferred brand sat on the end table beside her.

Mr. Crawford coughed and held out whatever it was he held in his hand. "We've been sorting through Sawyer's important papers and bills, attempting to finalize his affairs, and I found this."

All my efforts went toward not shaking when I reached for the paper. Though I hadn't laid eyes on its contents, I was certain about what it was—what it contained. Had he never told his parents about Harper? When she was born, I'd called him and left a message on his voicemail. Since he'd told me he didn't want the baby, I merely told him he had a daughter as well as her weight and length. I suppose a part of me hoped he'd come back, but he never so much as sent me a text message.

My fingers carefully opened the two panels, revealing the relinquishment of rights document Sawyer had sent me when I was pregnant. When we'd visited Elliot's attorney so he could adopt Harper, I'd brought the paperwork with me only to discover that the document wasn't legal. Instead, our lawyer now sought to have Sawyer's rights relinquished through abandonment. Since the document wasn't legitimate, it'd never occurred to me that Sawyer would've kept a copy.

"We want to know if you put our grandchild up for adoption?"

"I'm sorry?" I couldn't help that hysterical burst of laughter. Every cell in my body was squeezed so tight, I could have burst—something had to give somehow.

"We want to know if you put—"

"Forgive me, but I did hear you the first time. I'm simply trying to understand what right you have to walk in and demand that information from me."

"Since you didn't do us the courtesy of offering for us to adopt the child, what sort of response did you expect? We can only assume that you coerced Sawyer into signing that document, relinquishing his rights. Why else would he have become so different after your break-up?"

I threw my hands up and let them drop down, slapping my legs. "Oh, I don't know. Guilt maybe? I can tell you one thing. I never coerced your son into signing that form. I don't know who drew that up, but he had it delivered by what appeared to be a process server so I would be forced to sign for it. I only recently discovered that paper was a fraud." I clenched my hands to stop them from shaking. "If Sawyer changed after he left, it was due to his own demons, and not anything I imposed upon him." Yes, my voice was hard, but they hadn't asked what had happened. They simply accused without any foundation except the flimsy basis of their assumptions.

My phone buzzed in my hand and I lifted it. Elliot texted, "We're on our way to Gram's."

I slid the text open and typed, "No! Bring Harper straight home. I'll explain when I get there."

"We only want to know if we have a grandchild out there somewhere." Mrs. Crawford spoke with tears welling heavily in her eyes. "A part of him we didn't know existed."

"For what purpose?" I crossed my arms over my chest.

"We'd like to spend time with him of course," spluttered Mr. Crawford. "If a child was put up for adoption, we intend to discover where and sue for custody." He pointed to the form or me. I wasn't sure which. "Or if you kept Sawyer's child, we would seek visitation from you."

"Visitation?" My voice was hard. "On what grounds? I don't know much about family law, but if this child exists, I haven't kept you from it. Your son made the choice not to inform you of his or her existence."

"You could've let us know—" His father's face was reddening.

"I'm sorry, but how is that my responsibility? If Sawyer didn't want you to know about a child, then what right did I have to go behind his back to inform you? This was also over six years ago. Do you really expect to just take home a child who has no memory of you? How terrifying for that child."

Mr. Crawford stepped forward and leaned in. "Did Sawyer father a child?" His voice boomed through the living room and could likely be heard by anyone standing on the front step.

I took a deep breath and released my clenched teeth. "I do not say this to hurt you, but Sawyer was nothing more than a sperm donor. When I discovered I was pregnant, he suggested I have an abortion. I refused, so he attempted to persuade me to give the baby up for adoption. He signed and had that form delivered to me when I was six months pregnant. I've been told he couldn't terminate his rights as he did. I would've had to terminate his rights for abandonment, which I never thought to do. I wasn't going to force him to be a father. If he didn't want her, I did. And if you never knew of her, then it was never my place to tell you."

"He was her father." I hadn't thought Mr. Crawford's voice could get louder. I was wrong.

I raised my hand surely and quickly, even though my hand trembled, and pointed. "No, she has a father who has filed paperwork to adopt her legally. She adores him as he does her. Sawyer never so much as set eyes on her, and she has no memory of him. Was I supposed to tell her of a father who signed her away like he'd sold a car, and had done so before she was born—before he'd even seen her?"

Mrs. Crawford whimpered and sniffed. "A little girl?"

My gaze whipped to the picture that usually stood tall in Gram's bookcase. It was missing.

Mr. Crawford had been the minister at one of the local churches when I was growing up. I'd heard of his hellfire and brimstone sermons, though we'd never attended his parish. He'd also been very hard on Sawyer. I could only imagine what sort of anger Sawyer's lies inspired. I was always certain he was the reason Sawyer wanted to abort Harper or put her up for adoption. How likely was his father to forgive him if he'd known?

"We want to see her," said Crawford in a hard tone.

I shook my head and crossed my arms back over my chest. "Not like this. She's extremely shy and would be terrified of your yelling. I also won't have you telling her fairy tales of Sawyer. As I said before, she doesn't know of him, and I intend

149

to keep it that way for as long as possible. I don't want her believing someone didn't love her enough to be her father. I would never tell her if I had the choice."

"Well then! You'll be hearing from my attorney." He held out a hand for his wife. "Come. We have a phone call to make."

As soon as he'd stormed through the door, practically dragging his poor wife in his wake, Gram sighed. "He's always been a pompous windbag. I see nothing has changed."

"Do you think I'm wrong?"

"Of course not. You didn't close the door on them, but told them not right now. If he wants to make a stink about it, then it's his choice. If Sawyer hadn't died, they never would've known Harper existed."

I pointed above the television. "What happened to her picture on the shelves?"

"When I realized who was at the door, I pulled it down. It's in the drawer in my bedroom."

I don't know why them being ignorant of what Harper looked like soothed me, but it did. Perhaps it was Mr. Crawford's temper?

I scrubbed my face with my hands. "I need to go. Elliot messaged me and he's heading home."

"Call that attorney of his. You might need her."

After I took in a breath and blew it out long and slow, I hurried out the way I came. When I got into my car, I pressed the number to the attorney, Laura, on my phone and put it on speaker. I was put through right away when I told her receptionist it was an emergency. It'd been Laura who'd told me Sawyer pulled that stunt to make me believe he'd terminated his rights. She'd thought he'd been trying to escape child support. I'd been young and naïve at the time and believed his fraud hook, line, and sinker.

"Hi, Maggie. What's wrong?" When I heard Laura's voice, I pulled over into the parking lot at the grocery store while I sobbed and told her of the entire encounter.

"Can they do this? Can they force Harper to come stay with them? I know Mr. Crawford said 'visitation,' but I don't believe him. If I'd given her up, he intended to sue for custody. Why would I be any different?"

"Maggie, I need you to calm down."

I smeared the tears from my cheek into my hair with my free hand. "Calm down? How am I supposed to do that?"

"Because no family court judge will hand over unsupervised visitation to grandparents who've had no previous relationship with the child. Did you tell them the document was a fake?"

"Pretty much. I don't know if they believed that it was his idea or that it was not a real legal document."

"Okay, I need you to listen to me. We're going to need to hire an investigator. I have one I use for cases like these—"

"Laura, I don't know." I closed my eyes and shook my head.

"You can be certain their attorney will be investigating you for anything they can use against you. If there's anything you can think of, then you need to tell me now."

"There's nothing I can think of. They never liked me, but that wasn't anything I could help."

"What do you mean?"

I sighed and gripped the steering wheel a bit harder. "I don't know. Sawyer only ever said I wasn't supposed to go to his house."

"You indicated Mr. Crawford was extremely angry. Did he and Sawyer have a good relationship?"

"No," I said after a sniff. "Sawyer only went home to visit his mother and usually while his father was at work."

"See? That's what I mean. We need to get together and go over everything you remember. This investigator also needs to dig up whatever he can. You need to let me hire the investigator. This is to protect Harper."

I covered my face with my hands. "I keep seeing Mrs. Crawford's crying face. She perked up so much when she'd learned Harper was a girl."

"I'm not closing the door if they check out and they're willing to abide by your rules for visitation. I believe most psychiatrists would agree with your terms as well. It's the possibility that they might press for full custody or insist you're incompetent."

My forehead met the steering wheel as I groaned. "I hate this."

"I know you do, but let me do my job so you don't need to freak out this way. Okay?"

"Yes, okay." As soon as I'd set up an appointment for Elliot and me in a couple of days, she said my name one more time.

"Yes?"

"No matter what. Do not speak with them again unless I'm present. Got it?"

"Got it. Thanks."

After Laura said "bye," I hung up and composed myself enough to finish the drive home. What for fuck's sakes was I going to tell Elliot?

Chapter 14

In the end, telling Elliot about the Crawfords hadn't been incredibly difficult. Instead, holding him back from going after them was the problem. If he could've, he probably would've treated Harper as if she were Rapunzel, locking her in the tallest, most impenetrable tower he could find and throwing away the key.

The next morning, we spoke to the office at Harper's school, ensuring they were aware of a possible custody issue. Fortunately, the school staff reassured the both of us that they couldn't speak to anyone but us about Harper. We also removed Mei and Gram from the approved people to pick her up. We trusted them implicitly, but Gram couldn't protect Harper from someone who might attempt to take her by force and it simply wasn't right to put Mei in that position.

What I hadn't counted on was Mrs. Crawford sitting in the waiting room when I arrived at work. As soon as I saw her, I halted in my spot like a statue. "Mrs. Crawford, I apologize, but I've been advised by my attorney not to speak to you or your husband without her present. I need you to leave."

She stepped toward me, her red-rimmed eyes pleading. "I'm so sorry for the way my husband attacked you yesterday. When he found that document, he became like a man possessed. I think he wants to fix all the mistakes he made with Sawyer—be better for Sawyer's child than he was for Sawyer, if that makes any sense." Charlie, who at some point showed up in the doorway to the offices, drew my attention for a moment. She lifted her eyebrows in one of those expressions that spoke volumes.

"Again, I'm sorry, Mrs. Crawford, but I can't speak with you. If you need to talk to me, please contact Laura Wells. Her receptionist can set up an appointment."

I inhaled deeply and passed Charlie so I could escape into my office. The last thing I needed was to be tempted to say something I shouldn't.

"Maggie!"

"Mrs. Crawford," said Charlie calmly as I closed my door all but a crack so I could hear. "Maggie would never walk away if she didn't feel it was necessary. As her friend and employer, I ask you to respect her wishes or I'll be forced to have you removed from the premises by the authorities."

I quietly closed the door and pressed my forehead against it. How would Mr. Crawford react if Charlie had his wife arrested? A few moments later, a soft knock made me lift my head.

"Yes," I said, my hand gripping the knob.

"She's gone," came Charlie's voice through the door. "Can I come in?"

I pulled it open and walked to my desk, stowing my purse underneath. I had no reason to cushion the issue, so I simply said, "Sawyer died in a drunk driving accident on Thanksgiving."

"Oh, my God." Charlie whispered the words while she shut her eyes tight. "I hope no one else was hurt."

"No, he ran off the road. His parents believe it was intentional."

"So, what?" She crossed her arms over her chest and stepped closer. "His parents suddenly want to claim Harper or something?"

"Or something like that. They found that fake document he'd drawn up to relinquish his rights when I was pregnant. Apparently, he never told them about why we broke up or the pregnancy. They hadn't known she existed."

"Oh, shit." For someone who usually didn't care how loud she swore, Charlie whispered the last. "When did they contact you?"

"Yesterday. Gram called me here and insisted I come by the house. They'd shown up without any warning. Mr. Crawford insisted on knowing everything then became irate because I resisted telling him whether Harper even existed. He claimed he would seek custody if I'd given her up for adoption, yet he said if I kept her, they only wanted visitation. She's never met them, so I told them I wouldn't let them simply take her. I've also never told her about Sawyer. As far as I'm concerned, Elliot is her father, her only father, even if he hasn't officially adopted her yet."

I dropped into my chair, exhausted. "Mr. Crawford threatened to contact his attorney, so I contacted ours. This morning, Elliot and I spent the last hour ensuring the school would only talk to me or him, and arranging matters so we're the only two authorized to pick her up. She's going to report to the office at the end of the school day and not be released like the other students. That idea was Elliot's."

Charlie nodded. "It's a good one. If you need a babysitter, you know where to find us. I doubt they'd try anything in the home of one of Marysville's finest."

"That's probably true. I'm merely worried about how to afford this. I have a bit of savings for a new car, but the lawyer's hiring an investigator. I'd give anything to keep Harper from being hurt, but I worry about the bill."

"And that's what we're here for. If you're using Laura, I'm sure she wouldn't expect you to pay it all at once, and even if she did, Ellie, Jena, and I would be happy to help."

I covered my face with my hands and slid them around to the back of my neck. "But I can't ask that of y'all."

"You didn't ask. We'd do it anyway." Charlie put out a hand, palm facing me. "Don't argue. None of us are filthy rich, but if we pool our resources, we can help and hopefully, make a difference. Think of what happened with Ellie and Freya. She was terrified when William first discovered their daughter's existence. She'll understand how you feel right now. Don't sweat the money. We'll figure it out if you need help."

"Thank you," I said softly.

"Are you okay? Can you work, or do you need to go home?"

I covered my face with my hands and shook my head. I let my hands fall into my lap. "I need to work. If I go home, I'll go stir crazy wondering what if."

With a smile, Charlie stood and headed for the door. "If you need a baby cuddle, Wyatt's napping in my office. He's always happy to be spoiled some more."

"I'll keep it in mind."

She turned back to me for a second with a slight curve of her lips. "You do that." Then she returned to her office.

Harper had been begging incessantly since our return from Thanksgiving to buy a Christmas tree, so Saturday morning, I finally broke down and we planned a trip to the Christmas tree lot near the entrance of the Riverwalk.

Elliot had already prepped everything at home with a new tree stand and tiny, twinkling lights. On Friday, Gram gave me all of her ornaments since Amy Louise had decorations of her own. She'd seen no point in keeping them stored away when we could use them.

About fifteen minutes before the lot opened, we left. I had a small wedding to work that evening. I hoped arriving so early would provide plenty of time to decorate before I needed to leave for the church.

"Can we get a giant tree, Daddy?" I smiled while we swung Harper between us. She held each of our hands, and every three steps, we propelled her forward while she giggled. I had to admit that I adored it when she called him "Daddy," and lately, she seemed to say it constantly, like she couldn't get enough of it. Elliot certainly grinned widely like he couldn't get enough of it either. The two of them together made me swallow back happy tears.

"We'll have to see how big the trees are. We do have a ceiling high enough for one."

I'd been worried about the expense of the custody issues, but Elliot didn't seem nearly as concerned. Between the two of us, we did have decent incomes, but I still had anxiety regarding how quickly those expenses could add up.

When we reached the bridge, we climbed the steps to street level and crossed to the vacant lot across the street. Harper cheered and jumped up and down between us. "Do I have to hold your hands now? I want to run through the different trees to find the bestest."

Elliot squatted down and tweaked her nose. "Why don't you ride on my shoulders? Then you can see all the trees from the top and find the tallest of them all."

My rapid heartbeat calmed while he situated her above us. We'd been much more vigilant about letting her roam even a few paces in front of us. I hoped this would blow over quickly so I could give her a slight amount of freedom. We would've let her run through the trees before the Crawfords had shown up at Gram's door.

Before I expected it, Harper pointed. "I've found it!"

"Already?" said Elliot.

"Uh huh! It's beautiful!"

We picked our way through the lot until we stood before a tree that would fit in the living room, though we certainly didn't need one that size.

"Can we get it?" asked Harper in this breathy, awestruck voice.

Elliot smiled and put his hand up for a high-five. "You did good, Harp. Let's go pay. Would you grab that tag near the top?"

"Elliot," I said, my voice low so she wouldn't notice.

"It's fine." He leaned near to kiss my cheek. "The sooner we have a tree, the sooner we can have Harper at home." The words were whispered, but I grasped his meaning. He wanted her home where she was safe and sound, and I confess I did too, but I wasn't willing to shell out a small fortune to do it.

The owner of the tree lot didn't argue. Instead, he took the payment and wrapped it so it was easier to transport.

Harper started bouncing on Elliot's shoulders. "I want to help carry it!"

Elliot helped her down and showed her where to grab the netting somewhere in the middle while he grabbed the trunk. I picked up the top. "Ready?"

"Yep!"

We lifted and crossed the street. Fortunately, we didn't have to turn a corner for the stairs. But once we reached the cobbled Riverwalk, I took two steps and balked.

"Hello, Maggie," said Mr. Crawford with a rigid expression. His wife stood beside him, her eyes already latched on to Harper. It's not like Harper could be anyone else's. She was the right age, fairer than me, and sported that tell-tale ginger hair Sawyer inherited from his mother.

"Well, hello, sweetheart." Mrs. Crawford stepped closer to Harper, but my daughter backed up to Elliot until she bumped into his legs. He picked her up and held her to his side.

"Please allow us to pass." I straightened and stepped to the side in the hopes Mr. Crawford would let me continue.

When Mr. Crawford stepped after me, the tree suddenly became heavier and Elliot appeared at my side. "Take Harper home. I'll follow behind."

"You can't possibly—"

"Maggie, I'll be fine."

"Hi there!" Everything in me nearly sagged at the sight of Jensen striding forward, fully decked out in his uniform. "Mr. Crawford? Mrs. Crawford? I haven't seen you in forever. How are you?"

I made my break while I prayed Mr. Crawford wouldn't try anything in front of an on-duty police officer.

When I'd made it to the end of the brick pathway, Harper finally said, "Mommy? Who were that man and that lady?"

"People I knew a long time ago. Did they frighten you?"

She shrugged, and I set her down so she could walk. "A little, but I've never seen them before. Are they nice?"

"I'm sure they are," I said, glancing behind me. "But I really don't know them very well."

"You walked all fast, like they were bad. And we left the tree." She hadn't sounded upset until the last bit that went up in pitch.

I knelt down and took her hands. "Elliot can manage. In fact, I'd be willing to bet Jensen helps him get the tree to the house. Don't you think he'd do that?"

She nodded and tilted her head to the side. "Maybe Jensen and Aunt Charlie can bring Wyatt and help us decorate our tree?"

"Maybe." I straightened and offered her my hand, which she took, and I led her down the trail. "We can call Charlie when we get home if you want."

"Will I still get to hang as many ornments?"

"I don't think Wyatt is ready to hang *ornaments* on his own, do you?"

"No," she said with a giggle. "Wyatt is lucky to have a daddy when he's a baby. I wish I coulda had my daddy when I was little."

I would've squeezed my eyes closed if I hadn't needed to see the path in front of me. Damn the Crawfords! "You've never mentioned that before," I said carefully.

"I asked Gram once." She said it so casually, like it was a normal every day conversation. "She said the daddy God gave me couldn't be with us, and one day, you'd find me a new daddy."

"Did she?" Leave it to Gram to come up with that explanation.

"Uh huh. Is that what happened?"

We climbed the two steps to the stone patio, and I picked up Harper and sat her on the picnic table. I crossed my arms over my chest. "I suppose what Gram said is exactly how it happened, but I wasn't necessarily looking for your new daddy when I found Elliot."

I took a deep breath and squeezed my arms a little tighter. "I'm going to tell you something, but I don't want you to worry about it." Her little eyebrows drew together as she frowned. "If you have a question, you can ask me whatever you want. Okay?"

She nodded.

"That man and that lady were the parents of the daddy God gave you. Do you understand?"

"They were his mommy and daddy?"

"Exactly, which makes them your grandparents. You see, they only just learned about you, so they came to talk to me about seeing you."

She frowned and her bottom lip quivered slightly. "Did you say no? I thought you said they were nice."

I put my knee on the seat and set my hands on either side of her legs so I was closer. "I really don't know them very well, Harp, and I haven't seen their son since before you were born. He died, you see. He went to Heaven to be with God."

"Like Pop-pop?"

She never knew my grandfather, but Gram spoke of him enough that Harper at least knew of him.

"Yeah, like Pop-pop."

She didn't speak for a moment, but by the way her eyes gazed to the side and her quiet manner, I knew the wheels were turning quickly in that head of hers.

"You have to understand that Daddy and I want to be sure the Crawfords are nice people before we let them meet you."

"Is that why I have to wait in the office at school for pick up?"

I was always amazed at how quickly she picked things up. "For now. You're perfectly safe. Daddy and I are being cautious." The last thing I wanted was to frighten her, and I was worried that I was doing just that. "I'm sure they saw us and wanted to see you for themselves—to see if you resembled their son."

"What was his name?" Her voice was steady, thank goodness.

"Sawyer."

"That's a funny name," she said with a smile.

"I almost named you after him."

Her nose crinkled. "I'd rather be Harper. Otherwise, Daddy couldn't call me all those silly names."

Something about what she said made me breathe a little easier. "Very true."

A noise behind me made us both turn. Elliot and Jensen walked down the trail, carrying the tree between them. Elliot's jaw was tensed. I took Harper down from the table. "Why don't you run inside, wash your hands, and take that bowl of grapes out of the fridge? You can have your snack before we decorate the tree."

After she disappeared inside, I crossed my arms over my chest again. I didn't like the look on Elliot's face at all. "What did they say?"

"Mr. Crawford wasn't at all pleased that you whisked Harper away," said Elliot. "That man is a piece of work. He called you some lovely names before he tried threatening Jensen."

"I'm sure I wouldn't be surprised at whatever he called me, but how did he threaten Jensen?"

Jensen rolled his eyes as they climbed the steps. "Oh, some judge he seems to think he's friends with. Don't worry about it. I doubt he's as close to this judge as he thinks." He paused at the top when he was two or three paces away. "Look, if he continues to give y'all a hard time, get your lawyer involved and let me know. In the meantime, I'm going to file a report that I'll need you to come down and sign on Monday. That way, if this continues, your lawyer has the documentation needed for a restraining order."

"God," I said on an exhale. "I don't want to need that."

"No one does. I turned on my body cam when I approached so I have his scene on video. I'll be sure to upload it with the report. No family court judge, in his right mind, would even consider him close to being a suitable grandparent with what he said." He set down his end of the tree on the patio. "Call me or Charlie if you need us. We're always happy to help. After he shook Elliot's hand, he headed back down the trail.

"I can see the worry on your face," said Elliot, putting down the tree and taking me in his arms. "Crawford is an overblown windbag, but I don't want to underestimate him. We'll be fine—Harper will be fine."

"You promise?"

"Yes, I do."

Chapter 15

"Maggie?" I glanced up to Greta, who stood in my office door. She bit her bottom lip and her eyebrows drew together and lifted some all at the same time. I'd never seen that look on her face before.

"Is something wrong?"

"Well, sort of. There's a Mr. Whitaker out here with a package for you. He won't let me accept it. He says you have to sign for it."

My stomach clenched and twisted as I stood and carefully stepped around the door and into the entry. "Can I help you?"

"Ms. Margaret Dashwood?"

"Yes," I said slowly.

"Will you please sign?"

I quickly scrawled my name in the blank he'd indicated. He glanced at the signature then handed me a manila envelope. "You've been served."

"I wasn't aware that required a signature."

"My employer requires it as proof," said the man as he opened the door and backed out. "Have a good weekend."

"I should've told him you weren't here." Greta stood beside me, her face pale. Everyone knew of the Crawfords' attempt to see Harper on the Riverwalk. Of course, they all swore to keep an eye out for the couple around the office, but we hadn't seen them since Saturday.

"It's okay. Where I work isn't exactly a secret."

I took the envelope back to my office and hunted down Laura's work number in my contacts' list. The phone call took all of a few minutes since her receptionist told me to bring the documents directly into the law office.

After I hung up, I grabbed my purse and peeked around Ellie's door frame. "I have to run to Laura's. I was just served."

"Are you kidding?" Ellie set down her pen and straightened. "This has to be revenge for Saturday."

"Maybe, but what did they expect me to do? If they'd arranged a meeting and agreed to a few basic ground rules, then we could've set up a time for them to see Harper. I'm simply not going to let them tell her whatever they want about Sawyer."

"Have you told her?"

"After we ran into them on Saturday, I kind of had to. Apparently, she'd already asked Gram ages ago. Gram told her the daddy God gave her couldn't be there."

"That's certainly better than the truth."

"I agree. Besides, I think Elliot is a better father than Sawyer ever could've been—even at his best."

Ellie smiled and twirled her pen in her fingers. "It's obvious how much Harper adores him, and how much he dotes on her."

"I know. I love it. The way he accepted her without reservation definitely made it easy to fall in love with him." I scraped my teeth along my bottom lip. One of the sexiest things ever was how he interacted with my daughter.

"I bet it did," she said, laughing. "I'll be fine. You run those over to Laura's. I'll see you when you get back."

"Thanks, Ellie."

"No thanks needed."

With a quick wave to her and Greta, I left, dialing Elliot on my phone the moment my foot hit the sidewalk. After four rings, the voicemail picked up, so I took a breath and waited until it beeped. "Hey, I was served at work. I'm hand carrying the paperwork over to Laura now. I thought you'd want to know. Love you. Bye."

I hadn't changed into my tennis shoes, and Laura's building was on the opposite side of the park, so by the time I stepped into the reception area, my toes hurt from booking it in my heels.

"Laura's expecting you," said her assistant when she glanced over from her computer monitor. "You can go on back."

"Thank you." When I reached her office, Laura was eating.

"I hope you don't mind my sandwich. This is my lunch break."

"I didn't notice the time." I said absently.

She took the envelope and her forehead creased as she looked at me. "You didn't open it."

"I could only think about bringing it to you."

"I can't argue with that." She bent the clips forward and pulled the flap free of the adhesive. "Let's see what we have here." The papers were set flat on the desktop. Laura put on her glasses and began reading while she took a bite of her sandwich.

"They're seeking visitation under the claim that you've denied them access for more than ninety days."

"They haven't even known of her existence for ninety days. They showed up making demands, then attempted to ambush me on the Riverwalk. Did they expect me to welcome their unannounced encounter with open arms?"

"I understand completely. I need to speak with the investigator. The last time he checked in he claimed he had a lead he was following. Let me see if that information is something we can use. First thing Monday morning, I'd like to be able to set up a meeting with this attorney and the Crawfords and put an end to their suit then and there if I can."

"I'm sorry! I was with a patient when you called." I turned to Elliot standing in the doorway, completely winded and panting for breath.

"It's not a problem." Laura smiled and set down her sandwich before brushing her hands over the trash can. "I was just telling Maggie that I want to contact the investigator and set up a meeting with the Crawfords and their attorney. Maybe we can nip this in the bud without having to go to court. Honestly, given the circumstances, they don't have a leg to stand on. Their son didn't tell them about Harper, which begs the question 'why?'" She placed her hand on top of the court documents. "Leave these with me and go to lunch. I'll give you a call when I know something."

"Do you have any questions?" I asked Elliot.

"I don't think so."

"If you think of one, give me a call." Laura smiled and flicked her fingers toward the door. "Seriously, go have lunch and don't worry about this."

I gave a bark of a chuckle. "You know that's easier said than done."

"I know, but you're an excellent mother, and everyone in this town would testify to that. I can't see any judge in this state giving unsupervised visitation to grandparents who have had no prior relationship with the child—especially after six years." I nodded, even though my stomach still sat like a boulder in my belly.

"Thank you, Laura," said Elliot. "Would it look better if we were married?"

My head whipped around to him. My jaw had certainly plunged to the floor. Where did that question come from?

"Are the two of you engaged?" Laura glanced between us.

"No," I said quickly, "we've spoken of marriage as an eventuality, but that's as far as it's gone."

She let her chair recline back and folded her arms over her chest. "The courts always prefer married couples to unmarried, but that's not as strict as it used to be. The judge's beliefs can play a part though I wouldn't rush a wedding to impress a judge. My advice is to take your relationship at its pace, regardless of this suit." One side of her lips twitched up. "Besides, every woman would prefer a romantic proposal to a rushed marriage out of fear."

His hand wrapped around mine and he laced our fingers together, squeezing gently. "I would prefer that as well, but I don't have doubts so I'm willing, if it will make a difference."

She put her hand up, palm out. "Let me check in with the investigator before you go and rush what's supposed to be one of the most important days of your lives. Now, go take her to lunch, and you're not allowed to discuss this or a marriage proposal." She tilted her head down to give us both a not-so-evil eye over her glasses. "I'm serious. Now, go."

"Yes, ma'am," said Elliot, giving my hand a tug.

I let him pull me behind while I peered over my shoulder at Laura. "Thanks again."

When we were outside, Elliot drew me to walk beside him. "Sorry I didn't answer. I came as quickly as I could."

"You were at work. I wouldn't have been upset if you were too busy to get away."

"Fortunately, I was with my last patient before lunch." He swung our arms forward. "So, where are we going?"

"I should really get back to work."

"Come on, we can go to Starlight and grab a sandwich. They're always quick. Besides, Laura issued a direct order."

He wore this silly, endearing grin that made me sag a little when I took my next step. "Okay, I could grab a coffee for the caffeine to power me through the afternoon. I'm going to need it with all I have to do."

We skimmed the edge of the park until we reached Starlight. "Well, aren't you two just the cutest?" said Miss Bates loudly as soon as we walked inside. "It's been so lovely seeing you four girls find your handsome gentlemen. First Ellie, though I did worry when Freya was born with no man in sight, then Jena and Brandon. I knew about Jensen and Charlie before anyone else, you know. He came in here at opening with her coffee cup. It's not like anyone else in this town has a white, stainless steel travel mug with that particular Deadpool sticker on it." She clasped her hands in front of her chest. "And now the two of you." Her eyes zeroed in on Elliot. "I heard you're adopting Harper." Her voice sang it in that gushy way Miss Bates always spoke.

"Yes, ma'am. She's a great kid."

"It's so nice. Every child deserves to have two parents who love them. She's a lucky, lucky girl."

"I think so," I said.

Elliot's lips twitched up a bit on one side while he steered me to a nearby booth and sat beside me. Miss Bates followed from the counter, bustling in her bouncy gait. She set a menu in front of us. "What do you want to drink? You know the coffee and tea selections, but I also made a nice batch of homemade lemonade this morning."

"I'll have my usual latte." I nudged Elliot's shoulder. "What do you want?"

"Black coffee works for me, thanks." He passed the menu back. "I'd like the salmon wrap on a wheat tortilla if you have them."

"You know I do." Miss Bates looked at me as she tucked the menu under her arm. "How about you, sweetie?"

"Chicken and avocado on that homemade bread you have, please."

"Great choice. Let me know if you need anything else." She hurried back into the kitchen, the door swinging after her.

When I was certain the door was fully closed, I set my elbows on the table and propped my head on my hands, turned to the side so I could look at Elliot.

He simply rubbed up and down my back. "Everything will be fine. You'll see."

"It's a little hard to imagine at this point."

"Do you want to get married?"

I groaned and rolled my face into my palms. Once I shook my head for a moment, I turned back. "Horrible proposal

Martin. I'm with Laura. I'm not going to marry you for the sake of a court case unless it's absolutely necessary.

He nodded, but glanced down the table while he did. "Okay."

"Hey," I said, grabbing his hand. "Don't do that. I see us as long-term or you wouldn't be adopting Harper. But I want a real proposal, with you down on one knee, and at a time when it's not dependent upon my daughter and the Crawfords."

"I know." He lifted our joined hands and kissed my thumb. "But I don't like this. I told you how angry Mr. Crawford became that day on the Riverwalk. Jensen also mentioned his temper when we went into the station. Crawford threatened both of us. I just want you and Harper safe."

"I know, but let's give Laura the time she's requested. Everyone says she's a good attorney. Let her prove it."

"Yes, ma'am."

I smiled while he leaned in for a kiss on the lips. If only Miss Bates hadn't chosen that moment to return with our coffees! She, of course, gushed over our PDA, and I may as well have turned the color of the cherries on Miss Bates's apron, my face was so hot. Then, I stepped on Elliot's toes for laughing.

Tuesday morning, we sat in the conference room at Laura's office, Elliot's hand wrapped around mine. "You're fine. Harper's fine. We'll be great. Laura wouldn't have arranged this so fast if she didn't have enough to quash this stupid case."

"I wish she would've told us before we arrived."

"She explained that. Mr. Crawford insisted this meeting be first thing this morning. I simply wish I knew why."

"I think he's assuming we want to settle or we'll allow him what he wants," said Laura as she entered. "We don't have long before the Crawfords and their attorney arrive, so I need to ask you to do something for me. I need you to trust me. We may not be in a courtroom or in front of a judge or jury, but we don't have time to go over what the investigator found. Whatever I say, I need you to pretend you expected every last word."

"I'm not a great actress," I said, glancing at Elliot. "Can't you at least tell us the basics?"

"The investigator came up with a number of things—not the least of which was Sawyer's attorney, the one he used to draw up his will. Jonathan Hale, the Crawford's attorney, didn't sound pleased about his client's eagerness when he returned my call. Mr. Crawford wanted us to meet at their law offices, but I insisted on here."

The phone in the middle of the table buzzed, and Laura picked it up. "Thank you. Would you show them back?"

After she hung up, she turned to us. "It's been less than a week since you were served. I don't think any of us expected something to happen so quickly. I would've had you come in before opening this morning, but my husband had court and couldn't drop off our son."

"I understand," I said. "Harper needed to be dropped off at school too."

The door opened, Laura straightened, and we stood while the Crawfords and their attorney entered. As soon as they were at their seats, we all sat back down.

"Thank you for coming," said Laura in a very official tone.

Mr. Crawford's expression sent an odd and disturbing vibration up my spine. His lips had this ever-so-slight curve that reminded me of the Grinch. His wife's eyes set on me and Elliot before they latched on to Laura.

"Since the visitation papers were served, we've obtained some information I wanted to go over with both parties involved." Laura cleared her throat. "As the situation stands, the Crawfords are seeking unsupervised visitation of their granddaughter, Harper Grace Dashwood."

"Crawford," interjected Mr. Crawford. "Her last name should be Crawford." Mr. Hale casually placed a hand on his client's arm.

The interruption didn't appear to have fazed Laura. "When my client discovered she was pregnant, she told the biological father, Mr. Sawyer Crawford. We can prove Mr. Crawford was well aware of the child due to these fraudulent papers he had delivered to my client." She passed a copy of what could only be the relinquishment paperwork Sawyer fooled me with years ago.

"My client still contacted Mr. Crawford after the birth of her daughter, but did not hear from him again. We'd already begun proceedings for Mr. Elliot Martin to adopt Miss Harper Dashwood and had begun proceedings to terminate Sawyer Crawford's parental rights due to abandonment.

"We were, of course, investigating Mr. Crawford. After his death, the investigator located Mr. Crawford's attorney, who drew up his will as well as other paperwork, which included a notarized letter, concerning Miss Harper Dashwood."

She handed Mr. Hale a piece of paper. "As you can see by this notarized copy, Mr. Crawford claimed no rights to his biological daughter and cited his reason for abandoning her as a newborn—his parents. My investigator inquired into the incidents of abuse Mr. Crawford listed in Sawyer Crawford's letter, and we have police reports that document neighbors calling the authorities due to yelling and what sounded like hitting emanating from the Crawford's home when they resided in Marysville. We also accessed police records in regards to the Crawford's residence in Virginia and have found similar, very concerning reports."

Mr. Crawford slammed his fist on the table and shot up. "This is bullshit!" He towered over the table and us as he pointed directly at me. "You little bitch! You kept that child from my son and now you'll keep her from us if you can." He turned to his attorney. "I know what you said, but she's not a fit parent. I want sole custody of my grandchild. *My* wife and I aren't living in sin."

As he yelled, his voice grew louder and louder and his face turned a violent shade of purple as he continued to rant and splutter.

After he stood, Mr. Hale extended his arms, palms out. "Mr. Crawford, please calm down. We've discussed how your behavior can drastically affect your chances of ever seeing your granddaughter."

"If I listen to you, I won't ever meet my granddaughter. We said we wanted full custody, but you insisted the case would be thrown out of the courts, so we settled for visitation. I don't want visitation. I want my grandchild. She should be raised as a Crawford, and I'm willing to spend whatever is necessary to make that happen."

Mr. Hale groaned and covered his face with his hand, obviously giving up on tempering Mr. Crawford's rage. Meanwhile, Mrs. Crawford sat primly, her hands clutched around the handle of her purse, which sat in her lap. She didn't speak or look at her yelling husband, yet her eyes shone as if she might burst into tears at any moment. She had no visible bruises but that didn't mean she was well. How long had she let her husband walk all over her? Her situation at home had to be awful. After all, if the reason Sawyer had abandoned Harper was for her own well-being, how bad had his home life been? And why hadn't he ever told me about it?

Chapter 16

Laura and Mr. Hale struggled but finally managed to
remove Mr. Crawford from the legal office after Laura
threatened to call the police. When she returned, she closed
the door to the conference room behind her and leaned against
it. "I apologize for not mentioning any of this before. I know it
must've come as quite a shock."

"Sawyer abandoned Harper to keep her safe from his
father." I held the letter Laura had given to Mr. Hale, who
must've forgotten it with Mr. Crawford's outburst. As soon as
everyone had left the room, Elliot had snagged the papers
Laura had set out and pulled them over. I'd read over Sawyer's
letter twice during the furor. I still couldn't believe my eyes.

"Yes," she said. "He never mentioned his father's abuse
while you dated?"

"He mentioned his father liked to yell, but never
mentioned hitting. I never assumed he meant anything like
what we just witnessed. I was rarely around Mr. Crawford.
When we were in high school, Sawyer picked me up or we met
in the park. Once we went to college, Sawyer rarely visited
them." I leaned back against the table. "You know, I never
considered why at the time, but he always talked about how we
would leave South Carolina. He mentioned it once or twice in
high school, but when you're young, you dream about leaving
home, seeing the world. I hadn't thought about all of what that
would mean. When we moved into that studio apartment in
Charleston for school, he brought it up more and more. He
spoke of this idyllic life—like something out of a movie. I told
him I couldn't because I didn't want to leave Gram here on her

own. Being a short drive away in Charleston was an entirely different matter than being in Seattle or Portland."

Elliot squeezed my hand. "He wanted to run away, and he realized you wouldn't go with him."

"I first told him 'no' not long after we started college, but he kept bringing it up. He wanted to start plotting it all out: where we would live and work. I refused to discuss it. I saw no point in planning for something I couldn't do."

Laura sat in the chair Mrs. Crawford had vacated. "So, when you became pregnant, he cut the two of you from his life to protect you. If you'd married or they'd known of his child, you would be forced into a more familial relationship with them—tied to them for the rest of your life. You may have been subjected to his father's abusive behavior."

"But they moved before Harper was born."

"From what Sawyer's attorney told me, Sawyer graduated and moved to Chicago. His parents relocated nearby a few years later. That was when he contacted an attorney, who counseled him on custody issues. According to this attorney, Sawyer knew if something happened to him and his father discovered Harper's existence, his father wouldn't leave matters alone. Everything pertaining Harper was under lock and key in a safety deposit box. He must've missed that one document his parents found in his home."

I shook my head, my chest heavy. "I suppose he never really escaped. His father had described how Sawyer had changed after the break-up."

"If he'd met someone and had wanted to build a life with them, he may have made a bigger effort of breaking with his parents," said Elliot, shifting in his chair and resting upon one arm. "Since he didn't have that motivation, he stayed where he was. I feel bad for the guy."

Guilt ripped at my heart, but I'd had no way of knowing since Sawyer never told me. He never liked being weak. Perhaps he was ashamed. Whatever his reasons, they didn't matter anymore. I couldn't fix the past. At this moment, the best thing I could do for Sawyer was make sure his father didn't get one pinky on Harper. "What happens now?"

"They'd be fools not to drop their case. As Mr. Hale will inform them, we have enough between the police calls to their addresses to their son's wishes regarding the custody of his daughter. He intended for her to remain with you, Maggie, and whomever you chose to make a life with."

The vibration of my phone made me jump about a foot in the air. When I glanced at the screen, I frowned. "I'm sorry." I pressed the screen to answer and put it to my ear.

"Ms. Dashwood?"

"Yes?"

"This is Mrs. Holloway, principal at Marysville Elementary. We have a problem. The man you warned us about, Mr. Crawford, came to the school a few moments ago. He was really angry—so much so that my receptionist called the police while I tried to calm him. He insisted we allow him to see Harper. Of course, I refused. Unfortunately, he decided to leave right as Harper's class passed the office. They were returning from PE. He grabbed her so fast. We tried to stop him, but he ran."

"What?" I yelled.

"I'm so very sorry. Since the receptionist was on the phone with the police, they were notified immediately. It was chaos here." She sucked in a shuddering breath. "He knocked down several students as he ran out. Please understand that several of us chased after him. Her PE teacher included. I'm afraid he was injured in the attempt. He tried to open the car door to get to Harper. He was dragged down the road. We reported the license plate number as soon as we could." Her voice cracked as she continued to rattle out what happened so fast it was difficult to follow. "We're expecting the police any minute. I pray they find Mr. Crawford's car soon." Something that sounded like a sniff came through the line.

"Oh my God." I swallowed the vomit in my throat. Laura and Elliot had never removed their eyes from me. I covered the microphone. "Mr. Crawford went to Harper's school. As he was leaving, she passed the office, and he grabbed her. He's got her."

Laura immediately left the room while Elliot followed behind. "Thank you for calling, Mrs. Holloway. I'll be in touch with the police."

"I'm so sorry," Mrs. Holloway said on a sob. "If there's anything any of us can do to help, please don't hesitate to ask. We'd also be grateful if you could keep us informed. The children in her class are overwrought. The nurse is with them, and my vice principal is on the phone with the district to see if they can send over additional counselors. I believe any news of Harper would be helpful, even if I email an update to their parents this evening. I called you from my personal cell phone so you would have the number. Please call me at any time day or night—for anything, anything at all." A part of me wanted to rail at the woman, but by the sniffing on the line, she was crying and likely distraught.

"Thank you, Mrs. Holloway. Elliot and I will do our best to keep you up to date."

After a final thank you, she let me go. My hand clutched my stomach and I sucked in a huge breath to keep myself standing. I couldn't wither or curl up into a ball. Harper needed me. I lifted my phone and thumbed through my contacts until I reached Charlie's number.

The line rang twice before a laughing "What's up, buttercup?" sang through the line.

"Is Jensen around?"

"Maggie? What's wrong?"

I closed my eyes and gripped the back of the chair next to me. "Mr. Crawford took Harper from school. Jensen knows what the man looks like. I'd hoped he could help look for them."

"You know he will. Let me call him. I assume he can have your phone number."

"Yes! Absolutely!"

"Okay, give me five minutes."

I couldn't sit still after I hung up, so I followed the sound of Elliot's booming voice to Laura's office.

"Elliot! Calm down!" Laura pressed the screen on her phone and put it to her ear.

I immediately crossed to Elliot, pressing my hands against his chest. "She's trying to help, but we have to let her. I know you're upset."

"How are you so calm?" he asked. His entire body shook, and when he wasn't speaking, his jaw clenched tightly.

"Trust me, I'm anything but. I have to believe that Jensen will be out looking for her, and that he'll push his friends to search as diligently as he is. You know people on the force. They know we're together. It's also not a secret that you're adopting Harper. Don't you think they'll make this personal when they learn who it is?"

He closed his eyes and leaned his forehead against mine. "I would imagine they will, but it doesn't make this any easier."

"I'm not saying it does," I said. "I'm simply trying to keep you from ripping the head off of people who are here to help us." We turned at Laura's long exhale.

"I sent the police the best photos Elliot has on his phone. They've issued the Amber Alert. You have to realize how many people will be searching for them." Laura's phone rang, and she put up a finger while she walked to the other side of the room.

I took one look at Elliot, prompting him to pull me back into his arms. "Are you sure you're okay?" he asked.

"No, I'm not okay. He grabbed my little girl. I want to beat the shit out of him."

"Thank you, Mr. Hale. Miss Dashwood and Mr. Elliot will appreciate whatever help you can provide," said Laura, making me pull back and look at her. "I thank you as well." As soon as she hung up, she pressed her hands together, her phone still clutched in one of them. "Mr. Hale is searching property records for us. Since it's unlikely Crawford will take her to his home, we might be able to find a clue as to where he's taking her. You're welcome to wait here, of course, but you might be more comfortable with your friends and family."

"I won't be comfortable until Harper is with us," said Elliot. "I can't just sit here. I need to do something."

Laura put a hand on his arm. "The best thing you can do is stay out of the police's way. You have friends and Maggie's grandmother—"

"Oh God! Gram!" I pulled out my phone and hit send. I didn't want her to find out some other way.

"Maggie? Thank goodness!" Shit! Her voice was breathless. "I just saw an Amber Alert go across the TV with Harper's picture on it."

"I'm so sorry, Gram. Everything happened so fast. I didn't get to call you before that went up."

"That Crawford idiot did this, didn't he?"

"Yeah, he did, Gram. He lost his temper in the meeting today. It's complicated, but Sawyer left a will with instructions for Harper. He wanted to make sure his parents never got their hands on her."

Even through the phone, I could hear her swift intake of breath. "I can't believe it."

"We knew his father wasn't a good man, but we didn't know how terrible he really was."

Laura waved and caught my attention. "There's something for you in that paperwork. Don't let me forget."

"Charlie called and said everyone is gathering at the office," said Elliot. "They're arranging meals for everyone searching and want to be there for us. We should really get over there. Do you want to pick up Gram on the way?"

"You tell that boy not to worry about me. Amy Louise has already offered to take me wherever I need to go."

I covered my eyes at that no-nonsense tone from Gram. That was the voice everyone in the small town of Marysville knew meant business. "Okay, I love you."

"I love you, too, Margaret."

Once I'd hung up the phone, Laura held out an envelope. "This was for you with Sawyer Crawford's will and personal paperwork."

The letter sat poised in front of me while I blinked. Why did this suddenly feel like a nightmare? As Laura spoke everything slowed, becoming disjointed and odd. I watched my fingers close around the strikingly white paper while Laura's mouth started to move.

"You don't have to read it right now, but it has your name on it."

When I pulled the envelope closer, my name in Sawyer's familiar, bold, cursive handwriting was scrawled across the front. I nodded. "Thank you, but I can't. Not right now. I . . ."

"Put it in your purse and read it later." Elliot rubbed my back. "I think we should get back to your office. Charlie and the girls will worry." He shook Laura's hand. "Thank you for everything. You know where to find us if you hear anything."

"Of course," she said. "Please keep me updated. I'm sure you'll hear anything important before I get wind of it."

He wrapped an arm around my shoulder and steered me outside. When I stepped onto the sidewalk, I stopped to button my sweater. Elliot grasped my hand as soon as I fastened the last one and drew me forward. I didn't really see or register what was around me until I heard the ducks quacking away in the pond.

My feet simply stopped working and I turned. "Harper loves coming here." I shook my head and covered my face with my hands as everything sucker punched me in the gut. I folded over for a moment before I straightened and clenched my hands into fists at my sides. "Why did this have to happen?" I growled out. "Why couldn't Sawyer have shredded that document? He knew more than anyone what his father was like. Why would he take that chance? Why now?" With each question, my volume rose and rose until I was yelling.

Elliot grabbed me and pulled me towards him. "Shhh," he said.

"No!" I jerked back, throwing my hands out. "I don't want to be quiet. That bastard has my daughter, and I'm not going to be calm about it."

"Mags, she's going to be fine."

He was furious earlier. How was he suddenly so calm? "How can you say that? He has her! That man doesn't know a thing about her and he has her. Have you considered her allergy? He grabbed her coming in from PE, so she was taken without her backpack. He doesn't know she can't have nuts. What if she goes into anaphylactic shock?"

"Firstly, your daughter is a pretty strong-willed child. I think she'd be the first to point out that she can't eat something. Second, I read the wrapper of a treat I bought her the other day, and I caught her checking it before she ate it. We have to believe that she'll be okay. You heard him. He wants Sawyer's child. He wants a do-over. He doesn't want to hurt her. You have to believe that." He put his hands on my arms and lowered just enough to be eye to eye. "Don't forget that as far as I'm concerned, she's my daughter too."

I took a shuddering breath. I didn't know how to deal with this. For some reason, I'd managed to hold myself together at Laura's office, but now I was falling apart. I swiped a tear from my cheek. "I know. I'm sorry."

He pulled me to his chest and I inhaled deeply while he rubbed my back. The way my mood had fluctuated in the last half hour, he must've thought my hormones had boarded a rollercoaster that shifted between extremes.

"I think being with friends will help."

"I don't know how to deal with this."

His soft lips pressed against my forehead while I closed my eyes. "Who does? We just need to do the best we can and believe Harper will be back soon." That hole in my chest that was ever-expanding began to pull me down as I let out a sob. No sooner had it escaped than I pulled myself straight and drew away shaking my head.

"You can cry, Mags." His hands grabbed mine before I stepped back.

"No, if I let that out, I may as well be giving up, and I won't give up on my daughter."

"Letting out your fear and frustration isn't giving up on her." He stepped after me. "Crying won't mean you're weak. You're one of the strongest women I've ever met."

I dabbed my face with the wrist of my cream turtleneck and sniffed. "We should get to the office. Everyone will be waiting."

"They'll understand." His palms cradled my cheeks and steered my gaze to his. "Don't shut me out. Please." His eyes were pleading with me.

"I'm not—not consciously." I took his hands and held them between us. "I'm going stir crazy. Just like you, I want to do something but I can't, and even if I could, I wouldn't know what to do. I've never felt so helpless in my life." I released him and shook my hands in a futile attempt to get rid of the jitters as if I was being pulled in a million different directions all at one time.

"I can't explain it," he said, "but something in me feels like if we go to the office, there might be something we can do. I don't know. I can't imagine Jensen not keeping Charlie as informed as he can."

"I know you're right." I pressed my hand to my stomach. That hollowness was burning up my chest and closing off my throat. Elliot's arm slid around my shoulders as he steered me toward the park exit closest to the office. The last few days with Harper played almost like one of those old film projectors through my mind: riding on Elliot's shoulders while we hiked, him helping her with her homework while I finished dinner, the three of us making pancakes that morning.

How was I going to manage until Harper was found? I mean they had to find her, didn't they?

Chapter 17

Warm air bathed my face, which was cool from the walk, startling me back to the present the moment Elliot and I stepped into the waiting room at Forever Yours. Greta rushed around my old desk to wrap her arms around me fiercely. "Oh my God, I'm so sorry this has happened. I have a doctor's appointment I need to leave for or I'm going to be late, but I wanted to see you before I left. If you need anything, anything at all, call me."

"Thank you," said Elliot while I blinked, still a bit dazed. His hand pressed on the small of my back, guiding me while his hand clenched the fabric of my top, belying his show of calm. When he wasn't speaking, his jaw subtly moved as though he were grinding his teeth—another mannerism probably noticed by no one but me.

"There you are!" Charlie and the rest of the girls hurried into the waiting area. I didn't even have time to speak before Charlie set her hands on my shoulders. "Jensen wanted me to tell you he won't give up until Harper's found. He and his friends are all canvassing the routes leaving Marysville. He sounded so sure of himself. I'm hoping it means he has some sort of lead, but he didn't say that." She added the last bit quickly and held up both hands with her fingers crossed.

Jena shifted Charlie out of the way and gave me a tight hug. "Hopefully, someone sees the Amber Alert and recognizes her."

"William's closed up his office," said Ellie, hugging me after Jena moved aside. "He's going to pick up food and drinks on the way home. Y'all are coming over to the house and we're going to wait it out there. You know Jensen will call when he has any news."

I pressed my palm to my forehead. I had no desire to be sociable at the moment. "I don't know. I—"

"Don't you even!" Charlie stepped closer and pointed her finger in my direction. "You may have Elliot, but we're not letting the two of you go home. You have friends—both of you, and we're not letting you leave to deal with this all by yourselves. I've called your grandmother, and Brandon offered to pick her up on his way home from the clinic. Our dad is covering for him." Charlie looked back and forth between us while she lectured. Meanwhile, I peered over at Elliot. We both knew better than to argue with Charlie when she used that tone. "So, should we head over?" she asked. Her eyes continued to dart back and forth between us, waiting for one of us to protest. We both knew she'd never back down.

Elliot's hand squeezed mine. "I don't know if either of us is really up for a crowd."

I shook my head. "We appreciate this. We really do, but y'all have appointments and work to do. All of us can't abandon our clients for the day."

"Shit," muttered Elliot. "The clinic! I'm sure they've seen the Amber Alert on the television in the lobby. I need to call." He kissed my cheek. "I'll be right back."

Ellie lunged forward and grabbed my hands when Elliot walked away. "Look, after William checked out a project early this morning, he didn't have any client appointments and is perfectly happy working from home. While we would never mind closing down the office, Greta will be back after her appointment to answer phones. You know we keep on top of our clients, and yes, we have clients scheduled, but we have it arranged so only one of us needs to be here at a time. We've got it covered."

Jena raised her hand with a curve of her mouth. "I'm first shift."

"I'll grab Elliot when he's done on the phone," said Charlie, pushing me toward Ellie. "You two go and get settled."

Next thing I knew, Ellie grabbed my hand and pulled me out the back door into the frigid December air, our boots crunching on leaves that must have blown in from one of the neighboring yards. We usually kept the back courtyard and landscaping clean since we sometimes used the space for outdoor events—not that we'd had any of those since the weather cooled.

We entered Ellie's backyard through the wrought iron gate separating the properties. Ellie's husband William had purchased the enormous historic house before they married, renovating it and creating what could've been a showpiece for green construction in any architectural magazine. The location, next door to where we worked, made it easy for Ellie to go back and forth as she needed for her children.

As soon as we were inside her spacious kitchen, Ellie removed a bag of coffee beans from a cabinet. "I'm going to get some coffee going. I think everyone will need it to get through today."

"None for me, thanks. I don't think I can manage the caffeine. My heart rate is already too high."

She stopped and looked down at the crimson bag in her hands. "Oh, I hadn't thought of that."

"Someone is bound to want some. Please don't stop on my account." My heart already pounded against my sternum. If I added strong coffee to the mix, it might just burst from my chest. I knew from working with Ellie that it wouldn't take much for a spoon to stand up straight in anything she brewed.

At the slam of the storm door on the patio, I took a step back in time for Elliot to hurry into the room. "I'm sorry," he said, taking me in his arms. "I had to talk to the office manager. The receptionists had noticed the Amber Alert and recognized Harper like I thought they would. They were in the process of rescheduling my appointments with other therapists."

"Everything's okay, then?" I rested my forehead on his shoulder for a moment, inhaling deeply and letting his cologne flood my senses. Anything for some semblance of calm.

"Yes, the office manager was ensuring I didn't need anything."

"I'm making coffee," said Ellie. "Did you want some?"

Elliot kissed the tip of my ear before he drew back. "No, thank you."

"Yes, coffee," said Charlie, strolling in with Wyatt in her arms. "But I'll make it."

With a laugh, Ellie took a mug down from the cabinet. "How's he not bouncing off the walls with your caffeine habit?"

"Because I'm drinking decaf."

Ellie levelled a hard look at Charlie.

"Most of the time." Charlie gave a low chuckle.

With a roll of her eyes, Ellie shoved Charlie back and placed a filter into the unit, but before she could pour the ground coffee inside, the chime of the doorbell travelled through the house. "I suppose I won't be making coffee," she said as she headed toward the front door.

Charlie squeezed my arm. "That's probably a blessing. I still remember the first time William tasted Ellie's coffee. I thought he would puke." She cackled. "Are you sure the two of you don't need anything?"

"No, thanks." I shook my head.

"I'm fine," said Elliot.

"Oh my goodness!" said Miss Bates, who followed Ellie into the kitchen. "There you two are! William said you'd be here, but I thought you'd still be with the police." She set two portable coffee dispensers on the counter and clasped her hands in front of her. "When your little girl's face popped up on the television in the café, I nearly fainted, I tell you. I made everyone in the place quiet down so I could hear. The policemen sitting at table five paid right away so they could join the search, and when they heard I was bringing over coffee and pastries, they donated money to help out—so did everyone else in the café as well. Such lovely people." Her gushing trailed at the end before she perked up like someone shocked her. "These are caffeinated. I have decaf in the car with pastries. Mother is minding the customers, and two of my part-timers volunteered to prep trays of sandwiches for lunch, so don't you worry about a thing. I have it all covered!"

Elliot cleared his throat. "Miss Bates, you really don't—"

"Of course I don't have to, but that's what neighbors do!" She patted his shoulder before she bustled back out.

"People want to feel useful, like they're helping somehow," said Charlie. "We've been regulars at Starlight since we started the business. I'm not surprised she'd do this.

To be honest, I'm a bit relieved not to have to drink Ellie's coffee. Miss Bates's is lightyears better."

I attempted what was surely a pathetic smile while I crossed my arms and rubbed them. "I wish I knew what was going on."

"Jensen *will* call when he knows something. You know he will." Charlie's reassurance helped, but nothing could've taken away that nagging churning of my stomach.

Ellie's nanny entered the kitchen with Ellie's youngest, Jacob, in her arms. Miss Bates bustled back in behind her. "How he has grown!" Miss Bates put the next two large containers of coffee on the counter. When her hands were free, she took Jacob's small feet in her hands. "He's a cute boy! Yes, he is!"

The baby giggled and kicked while he kept his favorite thumb in his mouth, primed and ready to be sucked.

"I can manage for the rest of the day," said Ellie, holding out her arms for her son to be passed. "William should be home any minute."

The nanny nodded and passed over the child. "I'll see you tomorrow." She paused in front of Elliot and me. "My prayers are with your family. Please send word through Ellie and William if there's anything you need."

"Thank you," said Elliot.

The lady hurried out. Miss Bates returned a few minutes later with several boxes. When she opened her parcels, the scent of warm, buttery pastries filled the room. I simply wasn't hungry. I wanted solitude.

Without a word, I took Elliot's hand from my shoulder and tugged him into the living room. I pressed him to sit on the sofa, then sank onto his lap, nuzzling my face into the crook of his neck. It wasn't a perfect solution for my unease, but there wasn't much I could do. The only sure-fire cure would be Harper right there with us.

Elliot wrapped his arms around me while the fingers of one hand trailed up and down my arm. I closed my eyes and attempted a few deep breaths in a futile attempt to settle myself.

"I called Mom and Dad while I walked over. They wanted me to give you hugs and kisses from them. Dad offered to buy airline tickets for the two of them, but I told them to hold off. I didn't want them spending a ton of money they don't have—especially when we were flying them in for Christmas."

"I agree. It's not like there's much they can do here but wait with us. I'm not saying they aren't welcome, but their presence won't make matters any easier."

He sighed and pressed his lips against my temple. "I agree." The doorbell chimed and I groaned and sagged as far as I could into Elliot's embrace. Maybe I could block all of this craziness out for a while in order to regain some small shred of my sanity.

"Maggie?"

My eyes squeezed shut. "Yes?"

"Laura is here with a couple of guys from the force," said Charlie. "They need to speak to you."

So much for a moment's peace!

The hope that the gathering at Ellie's would remain small dwindled with each subsequent ringing of the doorbell. Mei arrived around lunchtime with a variety of Chinese takeout and an enormous rice cooker that was filled to the brim.

Ellie's husband William had eventually made it home close to lunch time with their four-year old, Freya, in tow. Jena's husband, Brandon, arrived not long after. Amy Louise showed up with Gram around the same time, and while Gram held my hand and doted on Elliot and me, Amy Louise joined Ellie's father and stepmother, who played with Freya and Jacob.

Micah, one of Ellie's good friends and our usual photographer, chatted across the room with Charlie while a television hummed in the background. Jena sat with her husband near the fireplace. The Taylors, Charlie's and Brandon's parents, arrived a short time before, laden with drinks and more food.

Giuseppe also remained after bringing by large pans of cheesy lasagna, salad, and bread.

"Sweetheart, you should try to eat," said Gram.

I stared down at our joined hands. "Why does everyone seem to think food will magically solve everything?"

"They're not stupid. They know it won't bring Harper back. It's their way of trying to do something. They love Harper too and feel just as useless. Don't be ungrateful."

I huffed and dropped my head onto Gram's shoulder. "I'm sorry. I'm not ungrateful."

"No, you're frustrated." She pointed to Elliot, who stood with William. He held a glass of water while the two of them spoke. "You and that boy both are. You think I don't recognize why you've separated yourself from everyone as much as possible today? I remember when that little Wickham mess hit

Harper in preschool. I thought I was going to have to bail you out of jail with how you went after his father in the principal's office. You're pushing all of that fury into a ball deep down inside and it's not good, Margaret. You need to let some of that out or you're going to burst."

"What do I do?" The words hissed through my teeth. "Rip Charlie a new one or tell Jena to go fuck herself?"

"If you need someone to shout at," said Charlie, making me jump, "you won't hurt my feelings. I honestly can't understand how you've remained so calm all day long. I would've been swearing, breaking things, and shredding everyone to pieces. Seriously, Ellie's shut down the office. If you need a verbal punching bag, let me know. We can sneak out back. My father has Wyatt under control." She tipped her head to Mr. Taylor, who snoozed in a recliner with Wyatt sleeping securely in the crook of his arm.

"Are you sure?"

"Positive," she said with a nod. "Come on, let's go."

Before I knew what was happening, we were outside, picking our way through the dark and up the steps with the help of the stingy light from a streetlamp along the road. When we were shut inside my office, Charlie faced me. "Okay, let's have it."

I shook my hands. "I don't know where to start."

"Pick someone. Do you want to yell at Sawyer? Mr. Crawford? Pick whoever you're maddest at and let 'er rip. Don't hold anything back." She shifted on her feet as if she were a tennis player waiting for a serve.

My skin prickled, being tugged in a thousand different directions. I scrubbed my face and raked my hands back to my hair, pulling and welcoming the sting.

"Come on, Maggie. I'm not Charlie, I'm Sawyer. I served you that fake document all those years ago and—"

"Why?" As angry as I was, the word was whispered.

"What?" She leaned forward and angled her ear in my direction.

"Why? Why did you never tell me?" The volume of my voice rose some.

Charlie's forehead creased, but she didn't miss a beat. "What did you think I should tell you?" Her hand landed on her hip.

"That your father was an abusive pig. That you knew he'd come after us! Why you always spoke of moving far away from Marysville to escape from him! You lied." My voice hit this low almost growl. My eyes stung and blurred. "Well, you fucked up! You left that stupid document where your father found it and now he has my daughter! My daughter, not yours! I'm the one who was there every time she hurt herself and every sniffle. You couldn't even be bothered to shred one fucking piece of paper! You selfish piece of shit! This is all your fault! If you weren't already dead, I'd kill you myself."

A door slammed and we both whipped around. "Maggie!"

Charlie frowned, walked past me, and opened the door to Brandon, who stood breathless on the other side. "What's wrong?"

"Maggie needs to come next door now."

My arms dropped to my sides, lifeless. I still don't know how I didn't vomit all over the floor.

Chapter 18

"What's going on?" Charlie asked while we hurried behind Brandon, who lit the path with a flashlight. "You need to tell us. The way the color drained from Maggie's face, I'm worried she might pass out before we make it to the house."

"You'll see. Elliot would've come, but he was busy."

"Busy with what?" When Brandon didn't answer, I jogged past Charlie and her brother while they bickered back and forth. Something was going on and I didn't have time for this, not when my daughter's life was at stake. I gradually sped up until I made it through the wrought iron gate and broke into a run, leaving it open for Charlie and Brandon to follow. I put my bodyweight into the back door as I opened it and tore through the kitchen. I froze when I reached the doorway. But how?

"Mommy!" Harper ran toward me and jumped into my arms. I barely had time to brace myself before I grabbed her mid-air. I couldn't stop myself from falling backwards and plopping down on my butt. I didn't release Harper. Instead, I clutched her to me while I started to sob.

After a few minutes, I drew back and ran my hands over her face, her hair, and down her shoulders, checking for anything amiss.

"She's fine," said Elliot, putting his hand on my shoulder. "Your grandmother and I both did the same thing the moment she stepped through the door."

"Yeah, I'm okay." Harper rolled her eyes and grabbed my fingers. "Maw-maw brought me home."

"Maw-maw?"

Harper glanced behind her, pointing over her shoulder with her thumb to Mrs. Crawford. I narrowed my eyes at the woman. She stood smack dab in the middle of the living room, her hands clasped together in front of her, as though she wasn't a part of this entire nightmare. I managed to get my feet under me and stood, hauling Harper up with me. There was no way I was letting my daughter down with that woman in the room.

"Woah," said Elliot, pulling me back by the hand still perched on my shoulder. "Before you go off half-cocked, she's the one who brought Harper back to us. Her husband will not be thrilled with her when he realizes—"

"I'm sure he figured it out when he found the car missing." Mrs. Crawford's shiny eyes met mine. "Please know this was never something I wanted to do. He threatened to kill me if I opposed him or tried to stop him."

"There had to be something you could do!" My tone was low again and dangerous.

"If I'd thought of a way before he'd grabbed Harper, believe me, I'd have stopped him. I didn't see an opportunity until we were three hours outside of Marysville. We pulled off for gas, you see. After Jarrod threatened me once again, he fueled up the car and went to the bathroom. He took his keys and the gun he usually kept under the driver's seat, but he didn't know I carried the spare set of keys in my purse. Once he'd rounded the side of the filling station, I moved over to the driver's seat, put my key in the ignition, and waited another minute to make sure he'd made it into the bathroom. Then I started the car and headed back in this direction."

"What about your husband?" Gram stepped up beside us.

"I called in an anonymous tip from my cell phone on the drive back. Hopefully, they have him in custody by now."

Someone bumped into me from behind. "What the ever-loving fuck?" I didn't have to turn around to know it was Charlie. "Thank God! How are you doing, Hardy har har?"

Harper grinned widely. "I'm good now, but you owe a dollar to the swear jar." With a grin, Charlie stepped around me and pulled out her phone.

"I've already called Jensen," said Mr. Taylor. "He'd been the first officer to arrive at the filling station in response to the 911 call. The clerk confirmed Crawford had been there but said he'd finagled a ride with an 18-wheeler driver who was headed back this way. They're searching that stretch of road for the truck. He radioed the station and they're sending officers over right now."

"Mommy?"

"Yeah?"

"I'm starving." Harper's overdramatic voice brought laughter from everyone.

"Well, you're in luck!" Giuseppe bounded forward. "I brought lasagna and bread. I know how much you love my lasagna." He rubbed his hands together with an enormous smile. "I even brought sfogliatelle, a yummy pastry from Naples—where I am from. What do you think?"

"Yes, please!"

Reluctantly, I set her down, but watched with an eagle eye as Giuseppe guided her into the kitchen.

"She's fine," said Elliot softly with a hand to my back.

I tore my eyes from Harper, settling them on Mrs. Crawford. "I'm confused as to how you found us here." I couldn't help it, but I shook from holding myself back. Mrs. Crawford could've saved Sawyer as well as Elliot and myself so much heartache if she'd had her husband incarcerated years ago.

"That would be my doing." Amy Louise stepped forward. "I ran by the house to take my medication and Mrs. Crawford and Harper were there."

"I knew where your grandmother's house was," said Mrs. Crawford.

My grandmother grabbed my hand. "Amy Louise had them follow her here. What Mrs. Crawford did was at great personal risk to herself, yet she did it because of her love for her son. Surely, you can understand." When I didn't answer, Gram stepped in front of me, put her hands on my cheeks, and tilted my head down so I would meet her eye. "Don't let your anger take over. You have Harper back because of her. You don't know what her life has been like for all of these years, so you can't know how hard it was for her to disobey her husband. Obviously, today was a turning point for her. Don't be unforgiving."

"It's okay." Mrs. Crawford shrugged with shiny eyes. "I read the copy of the letter Sawyer left regarding Harper while my husband was yelling in your lawyer's office. I always felt so useless when he was a boy. I'd never worked. I had no income. If I'd left, he'd have taken Sawyer, and I'd never have had any way of seeing him. I felt like staying was the best way I could protect him. I know that probably doesn't make sense to you, but it's all I knew to do."

The doorbell rang and Ellie hurried from the room.

Mrs. Crawford watched her leave before she turned back to me. "I'm so sorry. I know my husband hasn't made your life easy, particularly today."

Before I could answer, Ellie re-entered with Laura behind her. Laura's eyes widened when she saw Mrs. Crawford. "How?"

"Mrs. Crawford brought Harper back to us," I said.

Laura glanced at me one more time before she turned her attention completely to Mrs. Crawford. "What about your husband?"

"The police are searching for him." Mrs. Crawford clutched her purse tighter to her stomach. "I don't know where he is. The last time I saw him, he was heading into the bathroom at a Circle K outside of Charlotte."

"You're going to need protection." Laura pulled out her phone and started touching the screen. "I know of a battered women's shelter near here. We'll have to clear it with the police and the D.A., but it shouldn't be a problem." She put the phone to her ear and stepped outside the door.

I took a deep breath in an attempt to relieve that tightness in my neck. My grandmother squeezed my hand and I cleared my throat. "Mrs. Crawford, are you hungry? You may as well eat while Laura makes arrangements."

My grandmother squeezed my hand again.

"Thank you, but I'm too nervous to eat right now," she said. "I'm honestly relieved we had to come here. Jarrod won't know this place, and your friend, William, put the car in the garage to hide it."

Ellie tried to entice Mrs. Crawford into sitting, but she insisted on standing to one side while everyone buzzed around her. William had offered wine or beer to everyone to celebrate Harper's safe return, but she shook off every offer of food or drinks. When Laura returned, she was accompanied by several police officers. She spoke briefly to Mrs. Crawford before they disappeared into the foyer.

"Mommy, where'd Maw-maw go?"

"She's talking to Ms. Laura and the police." I pulled her onto my lap and cuddled her close. "Are you sure you're okay? You weren't hurt at all?"

"That man hurt me when he grabbed me and shoved me in the car because I kicked and hit him, so he squeezed me tighter. Once I was in the car, I was okay."

My eyes met Elliot's over her head. "What made you start calling Mrs. Crawford 'Maw-maw'?"

"I didn't know what to call her. She told me her name was Laurel, but I could call her Maw-maw if I wanted. You did say she's my grandmother."

"She is," said Elliot who squatted down until he was eye level. "The police will want you to tell them exactly what happened. Do you think you can do that?" She nodded and looked behind Elliot, prompting him turn as Laura approached.

"The officers in the foyer are taking Mrs. Crawford to that shelter I mentioned. I called and they've arranged everything, but before they leave, Mrs. Crawford hoped she could say goodbye to Harper." Laura's eyebrows rose as she silently implored me to say "yes."

Before I could answer, Harper began scooting off my lap. She took my hand and pulled. "Come on, let's go."

When Mrs. Crawford saw Harper enter, she dropped to her knees and took Harper's hands. "I'm very sorry about what happened today, but I'm glad we were able to talk on the way back. I loved getting to know you. You're a very special little girl."

"Will you take me to that zoo like you talked about?"

Elliot's arm slipped around my waist and tugged me closer. "We'll see, Harpsichord. Mrs. Crawford is going away for a little while."

Mrs. Crawford glanced at us for a moment before she nodded. "Hopefully, I won't be there too long, but whether we go will depend on your mommy and. . ." She peered up at Elliot and me. "And your daddy. Do you understand?"

My daughter nodded before she threw her arms around her grandmother. "Thank you for bringing me home."

Sawyer's mother all but crumpled as Harper hugged her tightly. Her eyes squeezed shut and she pressed her lips together. She took a deep breath. "I would never do anything to hurt you, sweetie. I only want you to be happy." Mrs. Crawford cradled Harper's face as she pulled back. "You listen to your mommy and daddy, okay?"

Harper nodded while Elliot put a hand on her shoulder to guide her back.

"Thank you," said Mrs. Crawford to us. "I'm ready." With a small wave to Harper, she followed the police outside.

"She isn't going to jail, is she?"

"No," said Laura from behind us. "They're taking her somewhere she'll be safe. I promise." She looked to us and clasped her hands. "I hope it's okay. With the custody suit done, I offered to represent Mrs. Crawford pro bono. Based on what the detective told me about that family, she's never worked and probably has no money of her own. I don't think she deserves to be prosecuted for this. Her husband is the real villain and she's as much of a victim as Harper and Sawyer."

"I don't mind at all." I heard the words come from me, making me pause for a moment and think. Yes, I really meant that. The notion surprised the heck out of me, but it was the truth. Gram was right. I couldn't know what her life had been like for all of those years. If Mr. Crawford's fury that morning was any indication, she'd likely put up with a great deal of abuse.

Laura gave a quick bob of her head. "Good! Now that we've got that out of the way. I need to speak with the two of you for a moment." She leaned over to Harper. "Would you go sit with your Gram so I can talk to your parents?"

As soon as Harper disappeared around the corner, Laura's eyes left the last spot Harper could be seen by us. "Two more officers should be here soon to take your statements," she said, her voice low. "Since we don't know where Mr. Crawford is, we need to find a place outside of Marysville for the three of you to hide out. I'm thankful y'all came here because the first places he's going to check are your house and your grandmother's. After that, he might try your office, which could lead him here. I know it's a long shot but still possible."

I crossed my arms over my chest tightly. "So what do you want us to do?"

"I might have an idea," said a voice, prompting us to whip our heads around to a woman standing on the stairs. "Forgive me. I was sitting with the baby until he fell asleep. I didn't want to disturb you, so I kept quiet." She climbed down the last few steps and held out her hand to Laura. "My name is Melanie Barrett. I'm Jena and Ellie's stepmother. I have a house down near Beaufort. Y'all are welcome to use it if it'll help. Jena and Brandon love to stay there. The property's not completely fenced in, but it does have a security gate along the road."

It was true. Jena and Brandon often traveled down to Beaufort for the odd weekend. "We wouldn't want to intrude." I shook my head. The offer was very kind, but from what Jena had said, the house was rather large and on the water. I'd feel guilty taking advantage of her generosity.

"Oh please! You wouldn't be intruding. I don't get there nearly as much as I'd like, and I love that the house gets used. I'll tell you the same thing I told Jena and even Ellie when she and William went there: simply leave the house as clean as you found it. They wash their sheets and towels and put them away before they leave." She lifted her eyebrows and leaned against the railing at the base of the stairs. "Your little girl will love it. I have all sorts of board games from when I was young along as well as some children's books. There's a great fireplace downstairs, and though the weather is chilly this time of year, you can still walk along the water and look for tidal pools."

"Are you—"

"I think it sounds amazing," said Elliot before I'd finished my question. "Thank you! Are you sure you don't want anything for us staying there?"

"Not a thing." Her smile was broad. "I'm just happy I can help out."

At the ring of the doorbell, Laura clapped her hands together. "Now that that's settled, let's get those statements made so we can get you out to Beaufort before midnight."

Chapter 19

I sat back in the porch swing at Melanie's house and used my foot to slowly rock while I watched the sun rise over the water. The marsh grass stood out in almost a silhouette with the backdrop of light and color coming over the horizon. After a sip of my coffee, I sighed.

Jena and Melanie were right. The house was incredible, and this small glassed-in portion of the porch had to be my favorite room in the house. In fact, the place was so great that I could almost forget that Jensen and the rest of the police were still looking for Jarrod Crawford. When we'd left, I hadn't thought the search would take such a considerable amount of time. How hard could it be to find one angry old man lurking around Marysville?

Even four days later, we received updates from Jensen on their progress. Laura had limited how many people were told of our location; however, the Beaufort police checked on us daily. From what Laura told me, they also patrolled near the house more frequently than usual since our arrival.

Crawford knew the location of Gram's house, so Gram had traveled to Beaufort with us so she wouldn't be at home. We'd also arranged for Amy Louise to visit her son and his family. Before we'd departed, we'd paid for her ticket and arranged for Mr. Taylor to drive her to the airport. We wanted to ensure she wasn't put in harm's way by remaining in Gram's house.

In the meantime, we waited. I hated waiting! I had weddings to plan and clients to meet, which was impossible from a couple of hours away. Ellie had rushed in to the office to get me a laptop before we left town, though trying to work from Beaufort wasn't nearly as effective. At Jensen's advice, we didn't go home for clothes or basic necessities, and William insisted we use his hybrid SUV to drive down, "just in case Mr. Crawford knew our car," he said.

I set down my coffee and turned the envelope from Sawyer in my hands. With the rushed trip to Beaufort, I'd forgotten all about the note he'd left for me with his lawyer. I'd rummaged in my purse for lip balm while I waited for the coffee to brew and its existence came flooding back into my mind.

After a deep breath, I ripped the flap open and pulled out a piece of legal paper folded into three. Sawyer's handwriting leaped from the page when I spread it open to read. As soon as I reached the end, I dropped it on the swing beside me and stared out over the water.

Two warm hands started rubbing my shoulders. "It's a beautiful view." Elliot kissed the top of my head. "I think I remember Brandon mentioning once how he and William converted this part of the wrap-around porch as a surprise for Melanie."

"The house was kept up, but houses like these always need work. From what Jena's told me, Brandon tries to fix some part of it as a 'thank you' of sorts whenever they come down."

His thumbs dug deliciously into the tense muscles of my neck. "I've been looking around to see if something needs to be done while we're here, so if you notice anything—"

"I'll let you know." I smiled while I looked up, bringing my hand to the back of his head and pulling him down for a kiss. "We're going to need groceries today." Ellie had filled shopping bags full of food from her refrigerator and pantry for us to bring with us. We'd protested, but she'd insisted because of the late hour of our departure. She also had no idea where we were going so she didn't know if we'd be able to immediately find a grocery store.

We'd gone out the first day and bought a few days' worth of clothes. Harper had been over the moon when we'd brought back new outfits and pajamas. Due to the recent Amber Alert, we kept her at the house. We didn't want anyone assuming she was still missing and revealing our location. Gram came in handy for that. She was also more than happy to remain behind, staying occupied with some crochet supplies we'd bought her.

"I'm going to grab some coffee and join you," said Elliot before he disappeared back through the door. When he returned, he settled in and took over rocking us while I turned and put my feet in his lap, moving the letter to make room. "Is that the letter from Sawyer?" At my nod, he lifted his eyebrows. "What does it say?"

I handed the paper over and sipped from my mug while he read. His eyes darted back and forth over the writing until he reached the end and let his hand fall into his lap. "For Harper's sake, I'm glad Sawyer wasn't the dickhead I originally thought, but I don't like that he was more concerned with how you'd see him than your safety—not to mention Harper's safety."

"I suppose I thought that he would've written something new, but aside from his pride being the reason he never told me about his father, he didn't say anything we didn't already learn from the paperwork Laura found. I'll save it for Harper, just in case she wants to read it one day, but Sawyer put me through enough. I don't need to dwell on this."

He nodded. "I agree. So, when do you want to go to the store?"

"I'm not in a hurry. They don't open for another hour or so anyway."

"The weather is supposed to be warmer today. We could walk." He caressed my foot with his free hand as he took a sip from his cup. "It looks like it's going to be a clear day."

"That might be awkward on the way back."

He shrugged and propped his cup on the armrest. "I wasn't thinking we'd buy too much. If we get a call that we can go home, then we'd have cold items to consider. I don't want the hassle if we can help it."

"You're right." I propped my chin on my hand. "Okay, we'll walk. I wouldn't mind the exercise."

"You act as though we haven't gone out for days. We walked along the water for an hour yesterday." A slight curve of his lips accompanied his light chuckle. "We can walk around a bit before we go to the store if you'd like."

"That sounds nice. I've lived in South Carolina all my life, but I've never been to any of these little coastal towns. What little I've seen is really pretty."

Gram padded in with her coffee. "Are you two going out?"

"We thought we'd go grocery shopping," I said.

"Good. We could definitely use a few things." She glanced between us. "The two of you should do something in town: get a bite to eat or shop. You've barely let Harper out of your sight since we arrived." I opened my mouth, but Gram pointed at me. "Don't get your panties in a bunch. I don't blame you in the slightest, but y'all can't forget to be a couple. Harper and I have enough food until you get back. I'm sure some place around here serves brunch or pastries and coffee. Get dressed, and I don't want to see you back until after lunch."

"Sounds like a plan to me." Elliot turned to me and wagged his eyebrows. "What do you say, Maggie? We haven't had a date in a couple of weeks."

He wore such a lighthearted, happy grin that I simply couldn't say no.

Elliot held my hand as we strolled down one of the side streets. Before we'd left, Gram had borrowed my work laptop and found a local place that boasted an amazing brunch menu. While we dressed, she'd even called to ensure we didn't need a reservation.

Even though Harper had been clingier since the kidnapping and suffered from nightmares, she still happily waved us off when we walked out the door. She'd been sleeping with Gram since waking us up screaming that first night after her return. Gram's presence was obviously enough to give Harper that security she craved and, in some ways, appeared to be dealing with the ordeal better than I was. The last time we'd gone out to buy a few things, Elliot and I'd hurried to do what we needed before we rushed back to the house as though she would be gone when we returned.

My arm touched Elliot's as we walked slowly, taking stock of what was in the windows. He'd insisted on buying me a warm woolen scarf in one of the high-end boutiques. I hadn't really needed one since I had a scarf at home, but the breeze coming off the water was cold. He hadn't wanted me to catch cold. We approached another shop, and he stopped, laughing at four fuzzy kittens who gamboled about in a large plexiglass play area inside the window.

"I wouldn't have thought you a cat person." I leaned further into him while a little black and white fur ball had somehow managed to scale the slick wall and was hanging half over the top.

"I'm more of a dog person, but I like most animals."

An older man stepped up to the kitten and carefully put him back into the shavings, a smile on his weathered brown face. He waved to us before he disappeared further into the shop. "Harper has been begging me for a cat or a guinea pig for the past year."

"Maybe we should get her one."

His remark was so off-hand, I drew away and pulled his hand so he faced me. "Now?"

"Yeah, why not." He ran his fingers through his hair. "I know a kitten wouldn't be the same as an emotional support animal, but it's proven that pets make humans happier. It's also been proven that they lower stress. I do think we need to have Harper see a counselor, but what if having a pet can help her? She can't sleep with Gram forever."

"No, she can't." I sighed. As much as I didn't want to deal with kitty litter or house training a puppy, he had a point. "Shouldn't we consider a rescue first? I've read horror stories about pet store puppies and kittens."

"You're absolutely right about that."

The man who'd waved to us from inside now stood in the open door. He lifted his hands, which held cleaner and a rag.

"Forgive me. I was coming out to clean the windows when I overheard your comment. We don't sell pets. Years ago, we sold fish and rodents, but my daughter didn't like the hassle. She runs the store now."

"Then the kittens aren't for sale?" asked Elliot with the most adorable dip to the center of his eyebrows.

The man leaned forward to glance into the window. "Those kittens were brought to me by a gentleman who begged me to find them homes. His mother's prize Maine Coon was 'violated' by the local Tom cat, and she'd insisted she had no time to deal with the mess. He'd managed to convince her to let the mother cat take care of them until they were old enough to be adopted, but she called him two nights ago to come get them. That little black and white one had escaped and discovered a roll of toilet paper. When they found him, he'd managed to destroy the roll." The old man laughed. "Her son refused to take them to the local animal shelter, so he asked me if we'd help out. He shops here for his Great Danes all of the time."

"That sounds like more energy than I'd like." I shook my head.

Elliot wrapped an arm around my shoulder. "Our daughter went through something traumatic. I thought perhaps a pet might help her."

The old man nodded and stepped back, motioning us inside. "Come on in. I think I know just the kitten for your daughter." After he set down his rag and spray bottle, he stepped over to the pen, reached inside, and pulled out an almost caramel-colored ball of long hair with tufts of creamy thick fur on her chest. "I've brought them home with me the last few nights. This one is playful but comes back to me to cuddle up and nap. She's a sweet thing." As his knotted, dark fingers scratched along the kitten's head, she leaned into the attention and began purring.

"What do you think, Mags?" He reached out and gave her little head a pet.

"I think we're going to have a difficult time keeping Harper from naming her Stitch." I pulled my purse further up my shoulder. "The problem is we haven't bought groceries yet and we still have to walk back to the house."

"Do you have everything we'll need for her?" asked Elliot. Had he even heard what I'd said?

"I can take care of her until you're ready. Just stop back by after you're done with your shopping."

"Do we need to leave you a deposit?" Elliot reached into his back pocket for his wallet.

"No, sir," said the man with a palm out. "The kittens are free to good homes. I promise not to give your daughter's kitten away. In fact, I have a kennel in the back room where I can keep her if you're worried." He turned his hand and leaned further toward Elliot. "My name is Jack. Why don't you choose the type of litter box you'd like and a few toys. If you'd like to bring your daughter in, she might enjoy picking those out herself."

He gave a few pointers on each item. We picked out a pretty basic litter box for until the kitten was larger. As I set a bag of food on the counter, a picture over the register stuck out like a spotlight. I leaned over the counter trying to get closer.

"Beautiful couple, aren't they?" Jack rounded the side and removed the thumb tack and pulled down the picture, passing it to me. "I met Jena last year. I met her now husband later. Do you know her?"

"I work with her." I startled. I shouldn't have told him that. "Please don't tell her we're here." I grabbed the man's forearm then jerked it back when I'd realized. "Forgive me." I glanced around. The store had no one but us, but I still checked. "My daughter was kidnapped at the end of last week. They haven't caught the man yet, so we're hiding out here until he's found. Jena doesn't know we're here. Only a handful know where we are."

He patted my hand before he wrapped his fingers around it. They reminded me of my grandfather's. They bore the same deep lines from age and were similar complexions. "Don't you worry about me. I won't tell anyone. Was that your little girl all over the television last week? The one with the red hair?"

"Yes, that's her." I blinked furiously to keep from crying. "We haven't brought her into town because of the Amber Alert. We were concerned someone might recognize her and not know she's already been found. My grandmother is at the house with her."

He nodded and patted my hand again. "I can see why you're considering the kitten. I hope she helps." He cleared his throat. "Now, if you'd like to bring your little girl in to look at the toys, I'll be happy to put the 'Out to lunch' sign on the door. You can even park behind the store and come in through the back door." He handed me a business card. "There's the phone number there. All you have to do is let me know."

"Thank you." I put the card in my purse.

Elliot walked up and set a box of kitty litter on the counter. "Is everything okay?"

"Yeah," I said, nodding. "It is." I handed Jack the picture. "Jena's mentioned you, you know."

Jack grinned broadly, his smile almost overtaking his thin face. "She's a good girl. She always visits when she's in town." He scanned the items on the counter. "How far away are you staying?"

Elliot lifted his eyebrows and I took a deep breath. "Where Jena always stays?"

"At Miss Melanie's?" At my nod, he chuckled. "When you get back from the store, I'll give you a ride out so you're not struggling. That's quite a walk with all of this. I gave Jena a lift out that way that morning she found Bacon. Did you know that?"

"No, sir, I didn't."

He pointed toward the door. "Now, you two get your shopping done. By the time you return, my daughter should be here to mind the store. I promise that kitten and I will be here when you get back."

"Thank you," said Elliot, taking my hand and leading me outside. As soon as the door closed behind us, Elliot glanced over his shoulder. "Do you think he's okay?"

"I do. Jena has said enough for me to know that she thinks of him as a grandfather."

"Good enough for me."

He tugged me down a few shops before we fell into our casual walk, peering into windows and behaving more like two honeymooners. As we passed a jewelry store, I paused and took in the different glitzy pieces that shone under the lights. Gram and I always enjoyed looking in the local jeweler's displays, and I always perused the cases while I waited for clients.

"What do you see that you like?"

One piece had caught my eye, but I wasn't going to tell him.

"No way. I know that expression on your face."

He tugged my hand, pulling me in the direction of the door. "Come on."

"Elliot, no."

The bell tinkled a greeting when we entered, and a sales lady jumped to attention. "May I help you?"

"Yes," said Elliot. "The engagement ring in the window. Can we see that, please?"

"Yes, sir. Give me a moment and I'll remove it from the display."

"Elliot, we aren't even engaged."

His eyes latched on to mine. "We could be."

"You're crazy." I couldn't help but burst out laughing while I said it.

"No, I love you, and I love Harper. I know you say we're already a family, but I want it all. I *can* wait, but why when we both know what we want?" He brushed a whisper soft kiss across my lips. "Marry me."

I closed my eyes and pressed my forehead against his. This was impulsive when you consider how long we'd been dating and how quickly we'd moved in together, but did that really matter? He adored Harper and was adopting her. He'd been my rock when Mr. Crawford took Harper. As terrified as he was, he held himself together better than I did, especially when I needed support. I also didn't want anyone but him. "Yes."

"What did you say?"

My eyes fluttered open and I smiled. "I said yes." His lips were on mine before I could say another word, and when he released them, we were both laughing. I wiped my eyes with my fingers as the sales lady returned and set the engagement ring on the counter. I had no idea how he knew this was the one that caught my eye, but it was exactly what I'd always wanted: a one carat brilliant cut diamond framed by smaller diamonds that almost gave it a floral appearance.

Elliot slipped it on my finger and I covered my mouth with my free hand. "It's perfect. It doesn't even need to be sized." After a quick check by the sales lady, she agreed and Elliot moved over to the computer with her to complete the sale while I continued to gape at my ring.

When we walked back out the door, I looped my arm through his. "How'd you know?"

"Because you looked at everything, but your eyes returned to that ring." He chuckled and slipped his free hand to hold mine. "I asked Charlie to keep tabs on anything you might like. She told the jewelers y'all work with, but they never noticed you lingering over anything when you were in their stores."

"Wow, you're sneaky."

His head jerked back. "Are you complaining?"

"Not at all." I held up my hand to admire my ring for the umpteenth time. "I love my ring. Thank you." I glanced around him at the bag he carried. "You didn't need to take a box for it, you know. I'm never taking it off." His smile was too big. "Did you buy something else?" I reached for the bag.

"No," he said, holding it out of reach. "I bought the matching wedding band."

"Oh, I want to see!"

"No." He shook his head. "Not until you say 'I do.' I want it to be a surprise."

"You suck." His rumbling chuckle made my tummy flip and then flip again.

Once we were inside the grocery store, he grabbed a basket and followed me down the aisles while I grabbed a few necessities, except instead of following me to the check out, he motioned for me to follow him down the wine aisle. "How about some champagne? We can get Harper a bottle of sparkling grape juice."

We picked out two bottles, completed our purchases, then made our way back to the pet store. True to his word, Jack drove us to Melanie's and helped us bring the groceries inside. Gram frowned when she saw him. "Margaret, what's going on?"

"You'll see," I said as Elliot entered.

The moment Harper's eyes landed on the kitten, she let out a squeal so high-pitched, I was surprised the kitten didn't bolt for the nearest hiding place. As it was, my ears would likely ring for the next few days. Harper carefully took the kitten into her arms and kissed the top of her head before she hugged Elliot. "Thank you, Daddy!"

"What about your mom?" he said laughing.

"Thank you," she said loudly before hugging me and kissing my cheek. "Thank you!"

Jack knelt down and held out a brush. "Now, it's very important that you brush her daily. Cats can get hairballs from grooming themselves and it makes them throw up. You don't want her getting sick, do you?"

Harper shook her head solemnly. "No, sir."

He handed her the brush. "Remember, every day, but be careful. She won't like it if you yank on her knots."

After nodding, Harper took the brush. "Thank you."

"Margaret, what's this?" At a plonk on the counter, I glanced up to Gram, her hand resting on the bottle of champagne with her eyebrows raised. Then her expression completely changed. "And is that what I think it is?" she asked, her finger now pointing to mine.

I bit my bottom lip and lifted one shoulder. "Probably."

Once we were both hugged and kissed, Gram refused to wait until after dinner to pop that cork on the champagne. Jack called his daughter to tell her he wasn't returning to the store before closing, and stayed for the celebration as well as dinner.

Elliot's heavy body dropped on mine and his labored breathing filled my ear. "I love you," he said, panting.

"I love you."

He lifted the sheet to roll off. "We're doing that a couple more times tonight, right?"

I laughed and curled against his shoulder. "For an old man you have high expectations."

"Ouch," he said with a hand over his heart. "That hurts."

At a buzzing from the nightstand, I propped myself on my elbow and let Elliot grab his phone. "Charlie, what's going on?"

I peered at the old alarm clock on my bedside table. It was almost midnight. Something was wrong.

"Are you sure he's okay?" He listened for a moment while I started tapping him on the chest. He grabbed my hand and held it tight. "Yes, of course. Just let us know."

As soon as he hung up the phone, I sat up. "Well?"

"Jarrod Crawford was caught attempting to break into Gram's house."

"What?" That sort of event was always in the back of my mind as a possibility, but it didn't mean its happening wasn't a shock.

"He pulled a gun on Jensen."

Suddenly I had a huge lump in my throat. "Oh, God. Tell me Jensen isn't hurt."

"No, Jensen shot Crawford first. He's been taken to the ER. Charlie doesn't know anything more." I sat up and wrapped my arms around my knees. "What's going on in that head of yours?"

"Is it horrible that a part of me hopes he doesn't make it?"

Elliot sat up and wrapped his arms around me. "If it is, then I'm right there with you."

Chapter 20

I startled awake with a sharp pain to my temple, making me jolt away from the car window with a gasp. My neck protested at what I can only imagine was the awkward position of my head while I slept. I rubbed that crick in my neck and moved my head back and forth. I must've fallen asleep rather early into the drive to Marysville. The last thing I remembered was entering the interstate.

"Good morning—again," said Elliot softly.

After another attempt at massaging the stiffness, this time from that point just below my skull, I stuck out my tongue in his direction.

"Mommy, that's not nice."

I glanced to the backseat where Harper sat with the kitten. "How's Lilo doing?" Thank goodness for Jack and the supplies he ensured we purchase. The kitten, Lilo as Harper had dubbed her, currently sat in a mesh carrier sleeping with her little back pressed against Harper's leg. I'd been surprised when my usually predictable daughter hadn't immediately named the kitten Stitch, but Harper had simply rolled her eyes. "Duh, Mommy! Stitch is a boy!" she'd said.

"She's fine but she wants out of the carrier so she can sit in my lap."

I raised my eyebrows. Harper had tried that excuse once not long after we'd been in the car. "She's sleeping. Besides, Mr. Jack said sometimes cats will try to hide in cars because they're scared. I don't want her burrowing where we can't reach her. Mr. Will wouldn't be too happy with us having to dig her out, especially if she rips something with her claws along the way. Let's leave her right where she is. Okay?"

"Yes, ma'am," she said with one of those almost growling sighs.

After Gram smiled, I turned back around in time to see the local high school as it passed. "We're almost home."

"We are. I'm taking your grandmother and Harper to the house before we do anything else. That way, they can get the kitten settled in while we take care of the police department."

As we turned onto the gravel road leading to the house, I tensed. When we'd spoken to Jensen that morning, he'd said the house was fine, but my heart beat frantically as we rounded the corner. What if Crawford had come here before Gram's? Had Jensen actually driven out to look or assumed? With all of that rolling around in my gut, I shouldn't have been surprised that the moment my eyes caught their first glimpse of the wood façade standing tall and apparently untouched, I sank completely into the seat.

Elliot helped Harper out and carried in the kitten while she followed. Gram headed toward the door with her shopping bag of crochet. Meanwhile, I opened the back of the SUV to start bringing in our clothes and what groceries we had left.

"Let me get those," said Elliot, removing one of the bags from my hands. "Go ahead and go to the bathroom or get a drink of water before we head into town."

"I'd thought about changing." I looked down at the comfy, grey leggings, soft white top, and chunky pink sweater I'd put on that morning. They didn't look terrible, but I wanted armor before we confronted what happened the day before. I needed this over and done. The last thing I wanted was to drag out these legalities for any length of time, but I didn't know how that would be possible. The kidnapping charge would require a trial, particularly since Crawford would never willingly plead guilty.

"If you really want to change clothes, you can, but I don't think it's necessary. Jensen asked us to meet him at the station. Laura may be there, but no one that you'll need a power outfit to impress. I'd like to get all of this settled sooner than later, wouldn't you?"

"Yes, I would. I suppose I'm not used to being so casual for something this official."

His index finger caressed my stomach through my top. "Once this is all over, I'd love a lazy day at home. We can call Giuseppe and pick up pizza. Gram can stay here tonight if she wants or needs to. Other than cleaning out the fridge and buying groceries, we don't have anywhere to be or anything to do."

"That sounds really nice."

He took the remaining bags, calling out over his shoulder as he began walking away, "Good, let's get this stuff inside and get to the station."

❦

Gram had offered to help Harper set up the kitten, so we quickly loaded back up in William's SUV and headed into Marysville. As soon as we arrived at the station, Elliot opened my car door and held my hand firmly in his while we climbed the steps and walked inside the police station. I don't know if he needed a boost but I sure knew I did. My stomach was turning over faster than one of those nausea-inducing rides at the fairgrounds on the Fourth of July.

"We're here for Jensen Worth," said Elliot when we reached the front desk.

"Martin!" When we turned, an officer I didn't know propped open a door. "Are you here for Worth?"

"We are."

"I'll show them back," called out the officer who held open the door for the two of us. Once we were all in the hallway, he walked on Elliot's opposite side. "I helped search for your little girl, you know. I'm glad everything turned out the way it should've. The entire precinct was willing to come in and hunt without a break until we found her. Chief was sending men home for a second shift, worried everyone would be flagging after eighteen hours or so." He gave a wheezing bark of a laugh. "Thank goodness, she wasn't missing for that long."

"We appreciate it." Elliot held out his hand for the officer to shake. "Maggie and I both wanted to be out there ourselves, of course, so we're thankful for all of you who searched for Harper on our behalf."

"Maggie, Elliot! Over here!" At Jensen's call, I left Elliot to continue speaking to the officer while I walked around several desks to Jensen, who was joined by a woman in a sleek charcoal pantsuit. "You must've left at sun-up to make it back so early." He gestured to the woman. "This is Emmeline Sims, the assistant D.A."

After I shook her hand, Elliot came up beside me and introduced himself. "Sorry, I was just finishing up that conversation."

"Nothing to worry about," said Ms. Sims. "Really, this is no more than a formality. Since you only arrived a moment ago,

I'm assuming you're unaware that Jarrod Crawford died at nine this morning."

I shook my head. "No, we had no idea." The tightly-woven bundle in my belly instantly released. I wouldn't want to wish death on anyone, but without Crawford, there would be no trial nor any threat of him returning for any reason. We were free and clear of him—forever.

"The D.A. and I are disinclined to prosecute Mrs. Crawford since she risked her own well-being to return your daughter. I hope you don't feel as if we aren't interested in your opinion, but we simply doubt—"

"I have no interest in prosecuting Mrs. Crawford." I glanced over at Elliot, who nodded in agreement. "She's been through enough."

"Well, then my job is done." Ms. Sims shook our hands. "I hope you have a lovely weekend." Elliot and I thanked her in unison. She picked up her briefcase and walked away.

Jensen watched her over his shoulder for a moment before he turned back with a quirk of his lips. "Now that she's gone, I'm sure you want to know exactly what happened last night."

I crossed my arms over my chest and leaned against the desk behind me. "Maybe a bit." Elliot's arm wrapped around my shoulders while we waited.

"Two nights ago, we had a 911 call that a man had been watching your grandmother's house. We made an extra pass and checked the windows and doors, but it was locked up tight, so I spoke with the captain. We decided my partner and I would take an unmarked car and park at the end of the alley to watch the house the next evening. A second car would hide in the back alley near the garage. I suppose Crawford was tired of waiting for one of you to show because at about nine p.m., he crept up the front steps and started jiggling the door. When it didn't give, he broke the side window and unlocked the front door to enter the premises. My partner and I called for backup and radioed to the second unmarked car that an intruder was in the house and that we were approaching from the front. When we entered, Crawford whirled around and pointed his gun at my partner."

Jensen sat on the edge of his desk. "I didn't hesitate. I aimed for Crawford's right shoulder. My goal was to disarm him, but I hit an artery. He lost a lot of blood at the scene before the ambulance arrived. According to the doctor who treated him, he began having seizures this morning before he finally went into cardiac arrest. They couldn't get his heart started again. I'm sorry. I really am. I wanted the bastard to go to trial."

"It's alright." Elliot clapped Jensen on the shoulder. "I don't know about Maggie, but I feel a lot better knowing he won't be able to harm anyone else. We don't have to worry about when his probation will come up or whether we can keep him in prison for a few more years. It's all done."

"Elliot's right. God forgive me, but it's an immense relief. I'm ready to go home and move on with our lives without dwelling on this for one more second. It's been difficult enough as it is."

"How's Harper holding up? Charlie and I have both been worried about her."

I sighed and squeezed Elliot's hand. "She's fine during the day. You'd think nothing ever happened. She had a nightmare on the first night after the kidnapping, so Gram slept with her after that. I'm not sure what she'll do when Gram goes home."

Elliot laughed and nudged me with his shoulder. "I think the kitten will help out, don't you?"

"You got her a kitten?" Jensen wore a large smile. "It's not exactly kitten season any more. I'm surprised you found one so easily."

"Pure happenstance." I shook my head. "I suppose it was meant to be."

Jensen nodded and shifted. "Anyway, you might want to keep your grandmother at your house for a few days. William's men are supposed to fix the window and put new locks on this afternoon." He held up a hand. "Before you argue, you should've replaced that relic of a lock a long time ago. William's putting in a much more secure system without your grandmother losing that antique wood door. We would've done it first thing, but we had to wait until the D.A. went over the evidence and made a determination before we could get a cleaning crew in there to take care of the blood."

I swallowed hard and fought a new wave of nausea. Gram would be bleaching every inch of the floors if she knew everything. "How bad is it?"

"Most of it was on the kitchen tile, so easily cleaned. The mats in there are ruined and the area rug in the living room should probably go. I think a corner of it had some tracking from the EMTs. If you tell us where to get a replacement, we can fix it up without her knowing any different."

I laughed. "Gram not know? You're kidding, right? That woman has a better nose than a bloodhound. Besides, those rugs were originally mine and purchased five years ago at Vernon Smiley's place on the old highway."

"And that store closed down two years ago," said Elliot. "We could always buy her new rugs for Christmas." His voice was so hopeful, but I knew my grandmother's reaction too well.

"We already bought her some enameled cookware since I took mine with me and she despises Amy Louise's. She'll have a fit that we spent too much." I scraped my teeth along my bottom lip. Maybe if we . . . Jensen, if you can get me a photo of the tag on the bottom of the rug before it's thrown away, I can search out the brand and pattern online and see if it's still made. What do we tell Gram in the meantime?"

Jensen shrugged and glanced back and forth between us. "Why not simply say we have to treat the house like a crime scene for the next week or two? Amy Louise is staying with her son until after New Year's, so we only have to pull the wool over your grandmother's eyes for a short time."

"That won't leave me much time to find a replacement." I'd have to get on the computer as soon as Gram went to bed.

"As long as we can find something close, she may not notice," said Elliot.

Again, I laughed. "You're talking about a woman who could tell by the look on my face if I was thinking of disobeying. Do you honestly think she won't notice a different living room rug? Talk about wishful thinking."

After a one shouldered shrug, Jensen glanced back and forth between us. "We could get lucky. I'll stop by and get that picture for you as soon as you head out. We're a few days away from Christmas now, so you could always guilt your grandmother into staying for that. I'll let you know when the mess is cleaned up. That way, if your grandmother needs or wants something from the house, you can go in and get it. You can tell her I went in for it or sent in a female officer if it's something that would embarrass her."

"Good idea." Elliot held out his hand. "Thanks for everything. We really appreciate it."

"No problem," said Jensen. "Any big plans for the day?"

"No." I shook my head. "After we trade William's car for ours, we're going grocery shopping then spending the afternoon at home. Melanie's place was amazing and a nice getaway for a few days, but I'm glad to be home."

"Look, call us if you need anything—anything at all." Jensen hugged me and shook Elliot's hand once more. "I suppose I'll see you at the Christmas party Ellie and Jena are planning."

"We'll be there," I said with a wave while Elliot pulled me toward the door.

When we reached the car, he pulled me into his arms. "What do you think?"

"That I don't want to think. I just want to go home."

"Then, let's go."

Chapter 21

The bed lurched and my eyes flew open in time to see Harper jump up and land on her butt right at my feet. "Wake up! Santa came last night!"

"You didn't warn me about this," mumbled Elliot, pulling a pillow over his head. I had to laugh at his frown when Harper yanked it away.

"Why are you so grumpy? You're never grumpy in the mornings." I wasn't about to tell Harper that was my fault, that I'd plied Elliot with Scotch then kept him awake doing wicked things to his body. Nope, that little nugget was going to stay tucked right up in my head where it belonged. What could I say? We'd put the presents under the tree and eaten the cookie put out for Santa. We'd tossed out the milk in favor of something more adult. After all, parents were entitled to their own Christmas celebrations, weren't they?

Elliot covered his eyes with his hands, rubbing. "Harpoon, why don't you feed Lilo? Your mom and I will be down in a bit."

I kept the sheets pulled up over my shoulders. "Is Gram awake?"

With a huff, Harper made the bed shake as she crawled off the side. "I already fed Lilo, and Gram's making cinnamon rolls."

"Go help Gram until we get downstairs," I said. "We won't be long. I promise."

As soon as the door closed behind her, Elliot pounced on me, making me squeal while he tickled my ribs. "You didn't tell me she'd wake before dawn. I should've cut you off last night."

I nearly snorted. "Like you would've."

"Okay, so I probably wouldn't have, and I'm not one to usually complain, but it was three in the morning, Maggie."

"You'll live, old man. You can do exactly like every other dad at Christmas and fall asleep after you eat a massive amount of turkey and stuffing."

"Old man?" His high-pitched cry joined his fingers in a new assault on my ribs.

"No, please!" came out in a gasp. "I can't breathe when you do that."

He swung his legs over the side of the bed and began pulling on his pajama pants. "Well, you shouldn't have called me 'old man'."

My shameless eyes latched onto his muscular back, watching while he finished pulling up his pants and padded into the bathroom. Why had I waited so long to give him a chance? We'd talked for months before he'd finally asked me out, but way before that, I'd known I wasn't unaffected by him. Now that we were together, I didn't want to consider what the rest of my life would've been if I'd continued to close myself off. "Does your grandmother always wake up this early on Christmas?" he called.

"Yes, her cinnamon rolls are a tradition," I said while I started to pull on my own pajamas. "She makes a big batch and has always walked some down to the police station. She hasn't mentioned doing that today. I know, initially, she'd planned to have them for all of us, including your parents, but with your parents coming for Easter instead, she's probably changed her plan." We'd had to reschedule the Martin's travel while we were in Beaufort. We'd had no idea when we'd return to

Marysville and didn't want to completely lose our money on the tickets.

I'd found the rugs for Gram's, but we didn't want her on her own. We were milking Jensen's excuse for why she couldn't go home for as long as we could. We only needed another week so Amy Louise could return from her son's.

Once we'd both brushed our teeth, Elliot pulled me into his arms for a kiss that had me clinging to his shoulders. I'd needed to do something to keep from melting into a puddle at his feet. I'd thought that feeling might disappear with time, but he still could knock me out of my slippers when he chose.

"Were you a good girl this year, Miss Dashwood?"

"No way." I sighed dramatically. "That would've been no fun at all."

He gripped my sides and dropped his forehead to my shoulder with a groan. "I say we open gifts then go back to bed."

"I have to help Gram cook. Remember?"

He took my hand and tugged me toward the door. "Let's go. The sooner we get the presents opened, the sooner we can find time to take a nap."

As soon as we appeared at the bottom of the stairs, Harper was bouncing on her toes while Gram set two large cups of coffee on the counter. "I told her to wait a little while longer, but she was determined and ran upstairs when I wasn't looking."

I gratefully took a sip of the strong brew and swallowed. "When hasn't she been determined?"

"Come on!" Harper grabbed Elliot's hand and began dragging him to the tree. "Daddy, you have to do Santa's job since you're a boy."

"How do you know I'm a boy?"

"Daddy!" Harper rolled her eyes and pushed Elliot to sit on the floor. I took a seat on the sofa and set Elliot's coffee where he could reach it.

He pulled over a large box and flipped up the tag. "To Gram, from Santa." With a grin, he pushed it in front of Gram's chair.

"You gotta do the next." Harper's incessant bouncing would make me motion sick soon if she didn't stop.

"Harper Grace, we're not going to rush this. You'll show some patience or you'll wait to open your gifts. Do you understand?"

Her eyes widened at my tone. "Yes, ma'am." I didn't want to take away her excitement, but she needed to learn to wait for others. She wasn't a two-year-old who we let open all of her gifts before we opened ours.

"Oh!" Gram straightened while she drew the paper back further. "You shouldn't have spent so much."

"Well, I hope you like them because I bought them on sale. I can't return them." I waited until Gram looked back down at the box of cookware before I let a sly smile peek through in Elliot's direction. I hadn't purchased them on sale, but I knew my grandmother. She was simply too frugal for her own good, necessitating an iron-clad excuse for why she couldn't refuse.

"You know I always thought you paid too much for yours."

"But you did admit they were the best."

Gram leaned forward and kissed my cheek. "I did do that, dear. Thank you." She kissed Elliot's and Harper's cheeks.

A small package was put in my hand. When I glanced down, I nearly choked. The box was the tell-tale size for jewelry. "We agreed we wouldn't buy one another gifts," I said.

A wicked expression lit Elliot's face. "I lied. I wanted to get you something."

"But I didn't get you anything."

He shrugged. "I don't need a gift. My Christmas gift is all of you."

Gram made a "tsk" sound and shook her head. "That boy's a silver-tongued charmer," she said, giving her hand a dismissive wave.

When I opened the box, I lifted a card from inside, a necklace with three white stones hung from the gold chain.

"It's nothing fancy. They're moonstones. I was passing that little vintage shop on the way to your office and noticed them in the window. I thought they'd be pretty against your skin."

He reddened a bit while he explained, which was adorable. I handed him the card. "Would you put it on me?" Once he fastened the clasp, I turned and kissed him on the lips.

"Eww!" said Harper.

Elliot laughed and shifted back toward the tree, drawing out a box decked out in Santa paper. I'd wanted to steer clear of toys since Harper had no need for more, so I hoped this would make her happy. She'd only been begging for this for the past year.

The paper was ripped off, and she yanked open the box, staring at the contents before holding up a black leotard. She lifted up a black wrap around skirt with her other hand. "Lu has ones like this for dance."

"Yes, she does." I pulled my feet up under me on the sofa. "But why would Santa give you dance clothes?"

Harper continued to pull out the contents of the box as Elliot picked up a card inside. The exterior had a Santa hat and when he opened it, he read, "Dear Harper, Your friend Lu told me how much you wanted to take dance with her, so I've arranged for you to go to the same class for the next three months. You'll need these clothes since Madame insists on everyone having a specific type of practice costume. I hope you enjoy learning ballet! Love, Santa."

Her eyes bulged. "I can take dance with Lu?" The high pitch of her voice made me relax.

"It seems so," I said. "What do you think?"

"I've always wanted to take ballet!" She started to slip the tiny pink satin shoes onto her feet. Thankfully, they fit perfectly.

"Sounds like Santa knew exactly what to do." Gram pointed under the tree. "But do I see one more gift under there?"

The last wrapped box was rather large so Elliot slid it out. His forehead furrowed and he glanced at me more than once. We'd only arranged for the one gift. Gram's wide eyes and fake innocence set off alarm bells. My grandmother typically gave Harper doll quilts or crochet animals. This was entirely too large and. . . were those holes in the side of the box?

Gram stood and helped Harper pull the top away while I held my breath. The lower box fell open and my daughter gasped. "A guinea pig!" Her little hands clasped together. "Look Mommy! Look Daddy!"

I hadn't needed Harper to tell me to look since my eyes had been glued to the furry little rodent when it opened. Now, straight ahead of me, was a fairly good-sized wire cage set on wheels. A smallish guinea pig sat inside chomping away at some food in a corner. I was going to kill my grandmother.

"Now," said Gram in her no-nonsense tone. "Santa woke me last night to let me know he put food for this little guy over there by your stocking. You need to make sure you feed him every day. Do you understand?"

"Yes, ma'am!" She dropped to her knees next to the enclosure. "I want to hold him."

"Not right now." Elliot shifted forward and started wheeling the cage toward the stairs. "Why don't we find a place for this guy in your room so none of us accidentally kicks the cage?"

"That would scare him to death."

Gram smiled at Harper's dramatic tone. "I think your daddy is right. Maybe on the side of your desk would be a good place?"

As soon as they disappeared at the top of the stairs, I set down my coffee. "Gram, how could you?"

"Quite easily. One of the ladies at church was giving away guinea pigs. Hers had babies, and she didn't have room to keep them all. This little guy has been handled all of his life so he's very good with children. The cage is on loan from her. One of the men from church is making me a habitat out of an old upright dresser. It should be ready next week, so I can return that one."

"Gram! I'm not mad about the cage. I'm mad because you knew I didn't want to get her a guinea pig!" The words were more hissed than loud. I turned quickly to make sure Elliot was keeping Harper busy for a little while longer.

"Margaret, did you see how happy she is? Elliot's done a marvelous job of loosening you up, but you need to relax more. I didn't give her a pony or a dog. Besides, you loved that bunny you had when you were little."

"This is more like a rat than a bunny." I shuddered.

Gram put up her hand, palm facing me. "Your dad had a guinea pig when he was younger. Harper saw the photo in my room after her teacher brought one into the classroom, and she asked about it. I also had no clue that you would get her a kitten before Christmas. I'd already spoken with my friend before the kidnapping, but afterwards, I thought, like you did with the kitten, that a pet might not be a bad idea."

"It will be a terrible idea if Lilo eats the guinea pig." I leaned back into the sofa, crossing my arms over my chest.

"Now you're being dramatic. If it's this much of a problem, I can keep the guinea pig at my house," said Gram in a tone I recognized easily.

"I didn't say that. I just wish you would've asked me." At the sound of someone coming down the stairs, I glanced back.

"That's a cute one," said Elliot as he plonked down behind me.

"Are you serious?"

"Well, yeah. Harper is holding him and petting him right now. I taught her how and showed her how to put him back in his home. I do think one of us should check to be sure it's latched, but she's over the moon." He peered over at Gram then back at me. "Are you annoyed Gram did this without telling us?"

"Well, yeah."

He smiled and shook his head. "We agreed she wouldn't have toys but experiences. A guinea pig falls into that category. I also think all of the distractions from what happened with Crawford are good."

"Next thing you'll be buying her a dog the size of a small house."

Laughing, he wrapped his arms around me from behind. "No, I think a kitten and a guinea pig are plenty. She'll learn responsibility and they'll be good emotional support for her."

I sighed and sank back against his chest. "I suppose I'm outnumbered."

"It'll be great," he said, winking at Gram. "You'll see."

A loud knock came from the door, and I set my coffee on the end table before I got to my feet. When I opened the door, Mrs. Crawford stood on the step, shifting her weight from foot to foot. "It's okay if you've changed your mind."

I stepped back so she could enter. "I haven't changed my mind. You surprised me is all. I didn't expect you so early."

"I woke while it was still dark out. It's been some time since I've been excited about a holiday." I took her coat and hung it from a hook while she gave a wave to the car in the lane. "One of the volunteers offered to drive me this morning. She also needed to get back to her house to cook. They have family coming over today." She clenched her hands together stiffly. "I can always take a walk if it's too early."

"No, forgive me. I'm not upset you're early. You're more than welcome."

She nodded and let out a long breath. "I really appreciate the invitation. I would understand if you didn't want me here."

I gestured toward the living room. "I think it's a good thing Harper has another grandparent, don't you? Besides, Christmas should be with family. I didn't like the idea of you being all alone in the shelter." Laura had told us that Mrs. Crawford decided to remain in the shelter for the time being. She was in the process of storing her belongings and selling the house she'd shared with her husband.

Once Gram and Elliot both hugged Mrs. Crawford, we all sat. A moment later, the pounding that always followed Harper on the stairs echoed through the house. "Harper! Stop running!"

"Yes, ma'am," she said as she reached the bottom. "Maw-maw!" My daughter did this incredibly awkward speed walk over to Mrs. Crawford and climbed into her lap. "Are you spending Christmas with us?"

"I am. I hope that's okay."

Harper nodded before she hugged and kissed her. "I have something for you." She climbed down and rummaged under the tree. I still had gifts for Ellie, Charlie, and Jena that she shifted to the side to draw out a small box from the back and set it in Mrs. Crawford's lap.

"Thank you," said Mrs. Crawford. "What is it?"

"A Christmas present!" Harper's voice held that tone that sounded more like she'd said, "Duh!"

"Harper," said Gram with a stern look.

She caved in on herself a little. "Sorry."

"I'm not upset with you." Mrs. Crawford took Harper's hand. "But your Gram is correct. The way you said that wasn't polite." After a glance at us, she smiled at Harper. "I was asking what's inside, but I suppose you're going to make me open it to find out."

Harper nodded and put her hands on the sofa cushion while Mrs. Crawford carefully began tugging at the wrapping. By the time she'd reached the tape on the bottom, the paper was still intact and probably could've been used again.

"Come on, Maw-maw, rip it."

"But I've almost got it open and the paper is still pretty." She used a long fingernail to open the last piece of tape holding it together. She carefully opened the box and pulled out the tissue, gasping when the contents became visible. Her eyes became shiny and she blinked madly. "This is wonderful." When she held up the picture frame, she pointed to the picture in the top left corner and tilted it so Harper could see it. "You look so much like Sawyer in this picture."

Harper had picked out the frame with multiple openings so there were spots for lots of photos of her. She'd wanted to give her grandmother memories from her life. Since I'd known Sawyer's name would come up, we'd discussed him and I'd shown her some pictures. I'd wanted to burn those photos after we broke up, but instead, I'd saved a few in the event Harper might want them one day. Harper now knew more about him, and her grandmother wouldn't have to walk on eggshells.

"He had red hair, just like me."

"And his red hair was like mine," said Mrs. Crawford. "Yours is somewhat darker and a color I much prefer to mine. I'm sure your mother's complexion helped out with that."

My daughter's little head tilted and her forehead crinkled. "Complexion?"

"Yes, your mother's darker hair and skin made yours not as fair as mine or Sawyer's."

Harper pulled at a lock, making it spring back up. "I get my curls from Mommy too."

"Yes, you do."

After Mrs. Crawford touched Harper's curls, she reached into her purse and pulled out a small bag. "It's not much, but I hope you like it."

When Harper pulled the gift from the bag, she gasped. "Earrings! I love them!" She wrapped her arms around Mrs. Crawford and gave her a bear hug before she hurried over. "Can I wear the unicorn ones? Please?"

"We'll need to clean them first, so why don't we take care of that after breakfast?" I gave the earrings a once over. Mrs. Crawford had done well. A pair of hearts and a pair of kittens joined the unicorns on the decorative hang tag.

Gram held out her hand. "The cinnamon rolls should be done by now. You know how much you love them warm. You can even help me ice them if you want."

"Yay!" Harper ran over to Mrs. Crawford. "Come on, Maw-maw! Let's go."

As soon as Harper iced hers, she carefully carried her plate to the table while Gram finished ours and put them on plates. She didn't come to the table immediately since she put another batch in the oven.

"That boy Jensen is coming over in an hour to take those to the police station for me. I hadn't expected him to offer, but it was his idea." She sat at the head of the table and held up her cup of coffee. "Merry Christmas."

⚜

Once Elliot and I loaded the dishwasher and Jensen had come and gone, Gram gave us both a shove. "Now, out! Harper and Mrs. Crawford—"

"Please call me Laurel," said Mrs. Crawford, "all of you. I don't feel like family should be so formal with one another."

Gram gave an authoritative nod. "Very well, Harper and Laurel can help me cook Christmas dinner. I want the two of you to go watch TV, take a nap, wedding plan, or whatever until we eat."

"But Gram—"

"No, buts, missy. Today, the grandmothers and the granddaughter make Christmas dinner."

Harper clapped her hands. "Yeah!"

Elliot grabbed my hand. "Don't argue. Let's escape while we can." His chest shook against my back from his laughter.

As I was being tugged away, I called. "There's alcohol under the sink in the half bath for Harp's earrings."

A dismissive wave was the only response I received. When we reached the top of the stairs, Elliot threw me over his shoulder while I giggled, tossing me on the bed as soon as we were in the master bedroom. He dropped onto the bed and pulled my back against his chest.

"I'm not sure you're happy enough about taking a nap."

His palm slid along my stomach. "I'm not averse to making love, but once I've caught up from last night."

My fingers found his thigh where it was draped over mine and pinched.

"Ow!" He grabbed my hand and held onto it while his arms held me tight.

"When do you want to get married?"

His lips caressed my shoulder. "Since you're asking, I'm sure you have something in mind."

"How about when your parents are here for Easter?"

"Can you put it together that quickly?"

"I can. I'd thought we could have it here. We could rent a series of tents or tables with umbrellas, depending upon the weather forecast, to go in that cleared area by the deck. I'll need to get the orders in for flowers and a cake soon."

He drew me around to face him. "I think that sounds amazing, but are you sure you don't want more—a church and a fancy reception?"

"Who says it won't be beautiful?" Did he doubt my ability to make simple ceremony lovely?

"I didn't say that. I don't want you to wish you'd had more."

I shook my head. "I won't. I never wanted anything big. Between family and friends, I think we'll be fine. If you want, we can make a guest list later today to be sure."

"Sounds like a plan," he said softly, rolling to his back and cuddling me to his chest. His fingers combed my curls back from my face as his lips found my forehead. "Maggie?"

"Hmm?"

"Thank you."

"For what?" I lifted myself up onto my elbow so I could see his face.

"For giving me a chance, for loving me, and for letting me be Harper's dad." He wore this serene smile that melted my heart.

I laid back down and draped my arm across his chest. "You don't have to thank me. You made falling in love with you so easy. You're the best father for Harper I could've ever imagined."

Epilogue

Charlie moved in a circle around me, fluffing my gown as she went. Gram stood nearby with her hands clasped in front of her. "You look beautiful."

I sucked in a deep breath and surveyed myself in the full-length mirror Emma had brought over from her bridal shop. I'd seen my dress in Emma's before Elliot had asked me to marry him and told Emma to make a note of it. Little did I know that Emma had set my size to the side. That woman must have had some sort of crazy premonition since, at that time, I hadn't even known I'd be marrying Elliot this fast. I mean we hadn't even been together for a year yet. When we'd first talked about marriage, I'd figured it would be a year or so before we actually tied the knot.

Strapless was a style I'd never considered for myself until I set eyes on the clean ivory wrap around bodice and layered organza skirt. Of course, the clear jeweled belt that separated the top from the skirt could've also been what changed my mind. Whatever the reason, I'd decided simply by seeing it on a mannequin. Even after trying on loads of other dresses, I hadn't changed my mind. Emma was the best. I owed her a huge one!

Gram had styled my hair in an up-do we found on Pinterest. I'd never straightened my hair and didn't want to do so today. We'd searched for a curly up-do I liked, and I'd gone over to Gram's on several occasions after work to test out different hairstyles to see which I preferred. Emma had also found a simple veil with a rhinestone accent that sat elegantly over the sort-of bun my grandmother had fashioned out of my thick curls.

I took another deep breath in the hopes those jitters in my stomach would magically disappear. My nerves were always set on edge for those weddings that seemed easy to plan, and this one had been extraordinarily easy. I'd never had a wedding come together with such little effort, hence the crazy butterflies. I shook my hands as Charlie came to a halt directly in front of me. "Stop that," she said.

"What?"

"I know you're not this anxious over Elliot since he's the best thing to ever happen to you. Therefore, all of this heaving you're doing is about the wedding." She put her hands on my shoulders. "I'm telling you now to stop it and relax. I went over all of the plans, and you didn't miss a thing. Greta has checked and double-checked the set-up downstairs. Micah's at the foot of the stairs with his camera, waiting." With all of the weddings in the Charleston area, I was relieved when our local photographer extraordinaire was free for the day.

Charlie snapped her fingers in front of my face. "You're not working your own wedding. Got it?" At my nod and eye roll, she lifted her eyebrows. "Ellie's at the top of the stairs, keeping an eye out, and I'm waiting on Greta's go ahead." She held up her walkie talkie before grabbing my hand as I reached up to touch my face. "Don't smudge the make-up." She shoved my bouquet into my hands. "Here, hold this instead."

While Jena was across town at another wedding, Charlie and Ellie were here as my matron of honor and bridesmaid. Both were decked out in sage green dresses, but in styles they selected while Emma ensured the colors matched. Meanwhile,

Greta joined them in ensuring the ceremony and reception went off without a hitch.

"We're a go!" came Greta's voice through the walkie talkie. Charlie had the volume entirely too loud.

"Alright, you two, we're ready." Charlie reached for her own flowers and beckoned us to follow her to the door.

I looped my arm through Gram's, and we walked into the hall. When we reached the top of the stairs, Gram slipped her hand into mine. "I'm so proud of you baby girl. I hope you know that."

"Of course, I do. You've never been shy about telling me."

"Not just your job or how you've raised Harper. I'm also proud of you for letting Elliot get close to you. He's a good man. I'm glad you're bringing him into the family."

"Mommy! Gram! Come on!" We laughed as Harper's voice echoed through the house.

"There goes the moment," said Gram with an impish curve of her mouth.

"Maybe we should do what Harper says."

Gram took the railing. "Let's get you married."

We slowly descended, one of my hands on the railing and the other holding my bouquet and my skirts so I didn't trip and do a header down the stairs. By the time we reached the bottom, Ellie was walking through the door while music from a string quartet filtered into the house. Charlie gave my skirt one last fluff before she made her exit.

"Do you remember how to drop the rose petals?" asked Greta as she knelt down to Harper's eye level. After my daughter's nod, Greta opened the door to let her out then turned to us. "I know I don't have to tell you what to do." She grinned and bounced on her toes. The music changed, and she gave a small squeal. "I hope you're ready."

I nodded and she opened the door. My hand rested in Gram's elbow as we walked across the deck to the platform we'd rented to extend it closer to the water. The few friends and family we had in attendance all turned to me, but since they were standing, I couldn't see Elliot. When we reached the beginning of the aisle, I turned, my eyes catching his.

He looked so handsome in his sleek black suit with Harper, decked out in her flower girl dress, standing in front of him with his hands on her shoulders. My smile grew until I probably blinded everyone. Gram led me down the four rows of chairs until I stood directly in front of him. After a few words from the priest, Gram kissed my cheek and sat in the front row with Laurel and Amy Louise.

Charlie took my bouquet and Elliot's hands grasped mine, sending my body into a shaking mess. This was it! I was marrying Elliot. I gazed into those devastating hazel eyes and used his soft expression to steady myself. I smiled and squeezed his hands in mine, making his happy laugh ring through the air.

Why had I ever fought my attraction to him? Now that I stood at the altar, ready to commit myself to Elliot forever, I recognized that since I met him, my mind had been overriding what my heart had been whispering: that Elliot had always been the one. He'd always been the one.

The End

Acknowledgements

What a year! We've all had a crazy run in 2020. When we rang in New Years last year, I never dreamed I'd injure my back, a pandemic, or an international move during that pandemic! I started writing this before the move and it became crazy difficult to try to finish. I had such a clear vision of Maggie's story, which I think eventually did come out despite my muse's distractions. I hope you enjoy Maggie, Elliot, and Harper, as well as catching up a bit with our other three couples.

My family always supports my writing endeavors. My husband did his best and still is trying to help me with my back. My children are inspiration when it comes to some of my characters. I never know when one of them will say something fun I can use. Brenna has even proofread my books.

Huge thanks to everyone from the online forums who have supported me in the past and now. Those were such important influences for me.

A giant thank you to Brenna and Debbie for proofreading!

I've had a number of betas and editors along the way, but Carol S. Bowes has stuck with me from the beginning, or nearly the beginning and was once again my wonderful editor. She's always a willing ear or eyes when I need an opinion on anything from a book, to a blurb, to a random blog post. She's a veritable walking resource that I can't do without.

The support of other authors is a great support system, as is the support and devotion of our fan base. Thank you to everyone who has purchased my books, left me wonderful messages, left an amazing review, and followed me after reading one of my stories. I wouldn't be able to have this much fun without your support and encouragement.

About the Author

    L.L. Diamond is more commonly known as Leslie to her friends and Mom to her three kids. A native of Louisiana, she spent the majority of her life living within an hour of New Orleans before following her husband all over as a military wife. Louisiana, Mississippi, California, Texas, New Mexico, Nebraska, England, and now Missouri have all been called home along the way.

    Aside from mother and writer, Leslie considers herself a perpetual student. She has degrees in biology and studio art but will devour any subject of interest simply for the knowledge. Her most recent endeavors have included certifications to coach swimming, certifying as a fitness instructor, personal trainer, and indoor cycling instructor. As an artist, her concentration is in graphic design, but watercolor is her medium of choice with one of her watercolors featured on the cover of her second book, *A Matter of Chance*. She is also a member of the Jane Austen Society of North America. Leslie also plays flute and piano, but much like *Pride and Prejudice's* Elizabeth Bennet, she is always in need of practice!

L.L. Diamond

www.ingramcontent.com/pod-product-compliance
Lightning Source LLC
Chambersburg PA
CBHW060150180626

46813CB00007B/2682